M. de Grafigny

Letters of a Peruvian Princess

with the sequel

M. de Grafigny

Letters of a Peruvian Princess
with the sequel

ISBN/EAN: 9783337383626

Printed in Europe, USA, Canada, Australia, Japan

Cover: Foto ©Andreas Hilbeck / pixelio.de

More available books at **www.hansebooks.com**

LETTERS

OF A

PERUVIAN PRINCESS:

WITH

THE SEQUEL.

Tranflated from the French of

MADAME DE GRAFIGNY.

TWO VOLUMES IN ONE.

VOL. I.

Cooke's Edition.

EMBELLISHED WITH SUPERB ENGRAVINGS.

LONDON:
Printed for C. COOKE, No. 17, Paternofter-Row;
By J. ASPIN, Lombard street, Whitechapel,
And fold by all the Bookfellers in
Great Britain and
Ireland,

LIFE OF

MADAME DE GRAFIGNY,

MEMBER OF THE ACADEMY OF FLORENCE.

MADAME de Grafigny was born in Lorrain, December 12, 1695, and died at Paris, in the sixty-fourth year of her age.—Her father, who by defcent was of the houfe of Iffemburg in Germany, in his younger days, ferved in the French army. He was aid-de-camp to Marfhal Bouflers at the fiege of Namur. Lewis XIV. in recompence for his fervices, made him a gentleman of France, as he was before of Germany; and confirmed all his titles. He afterwards attached himfelf to the court of Lorrain.

His daughter was married to Francis Huguet of Grafigny, exempt of the body guards, and chamberlain to the Duke of Lorrain. Much did fhe fuffer from the treatment of her hufband: and after many years of heroic patience, was juridically feparated from him. She had fome children by him, who all died young, before their father.

Madame de Grafigny was of a grave difpofition; her converfation did not difplay thofe talents which fhe had received from nature. A folid judgment, a heart tender and benevolent, and a behaviour affable, uniform, and ingenuous, had gained her many friends, a long time before fhe had any profpect of having literary admirers.

Mademoiselle de Guise coming to Paris to celebrate her nuptials with the Duke de Richelieu, brought with her Madame de Grafigny; and, but for this incident, perhaps she would never have seen that city; at least, her situation in life by no means gave her reason to think of it: neither had she, nor any of her friends, at that time, the least prospect of the reputation which attended her in that capital. Several persons of wit, who were united into a society, of which she also became a member, insisted on her giving them something for their *Recueil*, which was printed in duodecimo, in the year 1745. The piece which she gave is the most considerable in that collection. It is called *Nouvelle Espagnole; le Mauvais Exemple produit autant de Virtus que de Vices**. The title itself, we see, is a maxim, and the novel is full of them. This little piece was not relished by some of the associates. Madame de Grafigny, piqued at the pleasantries of those gentlemen on her Spanish novel, without saying any thing to the society, composed the *Letters of a Peruvian*, which had the greatest success. A short time after she gave the French theatre, *Cénie*, a piece of five acts, in prose, which was received with an applause that has continued to the present day. This play is one of the best we have of the sentimental kind.

La *Fille d'Aristide*, another comedy in prose, had not, on representation, the same success with *Cénie*. It was published after the death of Madame de Grafigny: it is said that the author corrected the last proof on the very day of her death. It is also confidently reported, that the ill success of this piece on the stage, contributed not a little to the disorder of which she died. Madame de Grafigny had that laudable

---

* A Spanish novel: Bad Examples produce as many Virtues as Vices.

regard

regard for her reputation which is the parent of many talents : a cenforious epigram had given her great chagrin ; and which fhe freely acknowledged.

Befides thefe two printed dramas, Madame de Grafigny wrote a little fairy tale of one act, called *Azor*, which was performed at her own apartments ; and which fhe was per- funded not to give to the comedians. She alfo compofed three or four pieces of one act that were reprefented at Vienna, by the children of the Emperor. Thefe are of the fimple and moral kind, on account of the auguft characters who were to be inftructed by them.

Their Imperial majefties, the emperor and empref, queen of Hungary and Bohemia, honoured our author with a par- ticular efteem; and made her frequent prefents ; as did alfo their royal highneffes Prince Charles, and the princefs Char- lotte of Lorrain, with whom fhe had moreover the diftin- guifhed honour of a literary correfpondence.

Madame de Grafigny left her books to the late M. Guy- mont de la Touche, author of the modern tragedy of Iphigenia en Tauride, and of the Epiftle to Friendfhip. He enjoyed this donation but little more than a year, for he died in the month of February 1760. She left all her papers to the care of a man of letters, who had been her friend for thirty years ; with the liberty of difpofing of them in fuch manner as he thought proper.

We may judge of the genius of Madame de Grafigny by her writings ; and of her morals by her friends : for fhe had none but thofe of the greateft merit ; and their efteem is her beft eulogy. The diftinguifhed marks of her character

were a senfibility, and a goodnefs of heart, fcarcely to be
paralleled. Her whole life was one act of beneficence. We
know but few particular circumftances relating to it; for
she never fpoke of herfelf, and her actions were covered
with the veil of fimplicity and modefty. We know in general, indeed, that her life was a continued feries of mif-
fortunes; and, doubtlefs, it was from thefe that fhe drew,
in part, that amiable and fublime philofophy of the heart,
which characterifes her works, and will make them dear to
pofterity.

IF truth, when it ftrays from probability, ufually lofes its credit in the eye of reafon, it is for a fhort time only ; but, let it contradict prejudice ever fo little, and it will feldom find favour before that tribunal.

What then ought not the editor of this work to fear, in prefenting to the public the letters of a young Peruvian, whofe ftyle and thoughts fo little agree with the mean idea which an unjuft prejudice has caufed us to form of that nation ?

Enriched by the precious fpoils of Peru, we ought, at leaft, to regard the inhabitants of that part of the world as a magnificent people ; and the fentiment of refpect is not very remote from the idea of magnificence. But fo pre-judiced are we always in our own favour, that we rate the merit of other nations not only in proportion as their manners imitate our's, but in proportion as their tongues approach nearer to our idiom. *How can any one be a Perfian ?* *

* The tranflator apprehends this fentence to be a fatirical repetition after fome other French author. There were a few firokes marked in the fame manner in one or two of the Letters, which he did not take notice of, as he fuppofed they would be unintelligible to the Englifh reader.

We

We defpife the Indians, and hardly grant a thinking foul
to thofe unhappy people : yet their hiftory abounds with monuments of the fagacity of their minds, and the folidity of
their philofophy.   The apologift of humanity, and of beautiful nature*, has traced the outlines of the Indian manners
in a dramatic poem, the fubject of which divides the glory
with the execution.

With fo much light given us into the characters of thefe
people, there fhould feem no room to fear that original
letters, which only exhibit what we already know of the
lively and natural wit of the Indians, are in danger of
paffing for a fiction.   But hath prejudice any eyes ? There
is no fecurity againft its judgment, and we fhould have been
careful not to fubmit this work to it, if its empire had been
without bounds.   It feems needlefs to give notice, that the
firft letters of Zilia were tranflated by herfelf : every one muft
eafily judge, that, being compofed in a language, and traced
in a manner equally unknown to us, this collection could
never have reached us, if the fame hand had not written
them over in our tongue.

We owe this tranflation to Zilia's leifure in her retreat:
her complaifance in communicating them to the Chevalier
Deterville, and the permiffion he at laft obtained to keep
them, were the means that conveyed them into our hands.

* M. de Voltaire.

It

It will eafily be feen, by the peculiarity of ftyle, that we have been fcrupuloufly careful not to take away any thing of the genuine fpirit that reigns in this work. We have been content with fuppreffing (efpecially in the firft letters) a great number of Oriental* terms and comparifons, which efcaped Zilia, though fhe knew the French tongue perfectly well when fhe tranflated them : we have only left fo many of them as may fhew the neceffity of retrenching the reft. We thought it poffible alfo to give a more intelligible turn to certain metaphyfical ftrokes, which might have appeared obfcure ; but this we have done without changing the thought itfelf. This is the only part that the editor has had in this fingular work.

* The French editor here ufes Oriental, for lofty and fwelling, though the Peruvians, with refpect to us, are certainly an Occidental people.

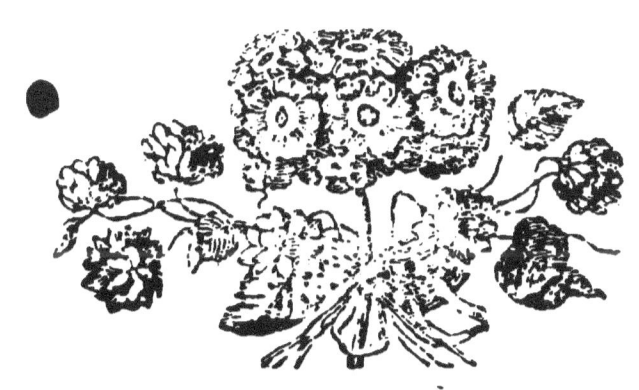

APOLOGY.

To what the editor hath already faid, the tranflator begs leave to add, that, as he went through his tafk with peculiar pleafure, he hopes he has done juftice to a work which appears to him to have great beauty in the original. The Peruvian character, as far as we know it from hiftory, joined to that of good fenfe, inflexible virtue, tender fentiments, and unchangeable affections, cannot be more ftrongly and naturally painted than in the letters of Zilia ; nor do we often fee the progrefs of the human mind fo correctly and expreffively drawn as in thefe letters.

To this edition are now firft added the letters of Aza ; the advertifement prefixed to them, by the French editor, fhews by what means they were obtained. We fhall only add here, that by thefe letters the hiftory of Aza and Zilia is rendered complete. We prefume, moreover, that in the force and turns of paffion, in delicacy of fentiment, in variety of incidents, in pertinent reflections, and in dignity, propriety, and elegance of expreffion, they will not be found inferior to the moft admired among the letters of Zilia.

AN HISTORICAL INTRODUCTION

TO THE

PERUVIAN LETTERS.

THERE is no people, the knowledge of whofe origin and antiquities is more confined than that of the Peruvians. Their annals fcarcely contain the hiftory of four centuries.

Marcccapac, according to the tradition of thefe people, was their legiflator, and their firft Inca. The Sun, whom they call their father, and regard as a god, touched, they fay, with that barbarity in which they had for a long time lived, fent them from heaven two of his children, a fon and a daughter, who were to give them laws, and to induce them, by cultivating the earth, and raifing of cities, to become rational beings.. It was therefore to *Marccapac* and to his wife *Coya Mama Oello Huaco,* that the Peruvians owed thofe principles, thofe manners and arts, by which they were made a happy people : before avarice, iffuing from a world, of whofe exiftence they had no idea, brought tyrants to their land, whofe barbarity was a difgrace to human nature, and the peculiar infamy of the age in which they lived.

The particular situation of the Peruvians at the time the Spaniards made their descent, was the most favourable to the latter that can be conceived. There had been, for some time past, a report of an oracle which had declared, " That after a certain number of kings' reigns, there should arrive in that country a wonderful sort of men, such as had never yet been seen, who should usurp their government, and destroy their religion."

Though astronomy was one of the chief sciences among the Peruvians, they were yet as much frightened by prodigies as other nations. Three circles that were seen round the moon; but especially certain comets which then appeared; an eagle pursued by other birds; the sea that overflowed its bounds; all made the predictions of the oracle to appear as infallible as they were fatal.

The eldest son of the seventh Inca, whose name*, in the Peruvian language, declared the fatality of his speech, had formerly seen a figure quite different from that of the Peruvians. A robe covered the spectre quite to the feet; he had a long beard, and was seated on an unknown animal, which he governed. All this astonished the young prince, to whom the fantom declared that he was descended from the Sun, was the brother of Mancocapac, and that he was called Virachocha.

* *Yahuarhuacac*, which literally signifies *Bloody Tears*.

This

This ridiculous ſtory had been unluckily preſerved among the Peruvians, and when they ſaw the Spaniards with long beards, their limbs covered, and mounted on animals they had never before ſeen, they took them to be the children of Viracocha, who called himſelf the offspring of the Sun ; and from thence it came that the uſurper aſſumed, by the ambaſſadors he ſent among them, the title of the deſcendant from the god they adored. All things bowed before the conquerors. Mankind are every where the ſame. The Spaniards were almoſt generally acknowledged as a kind of gods, whoſe wrath was not to be appeaſed by the moſt pro-tuſe offerings, nor the moſt abject humiliation.

The Peruvians perceiving that the horſes of the Spaniards champed their bits, imagined that thoſe tractable monſters, who partook of their reſpect, and perhaps their worſhip, were nouriſhed by that metal. They therefore daily brought a vaſt quantity of gold and ſilver, and laid it before them, by way of offering. We mention this circumſtance merely to ſhew the credulity of the Peruvians, and the facility with which the Spaniards were enabled to ſubdue them.

Whatever homage the Peruvians might render the ty-rants, they had diſplayed too much of their riches ever to have any ſort of indulgence from them. A whole people, ſubmiſſive and ſupplicating mercy, were put to the ſword.

B

By

By the violation of every law of humanity, the Spaniards became abfolute mafters of all the treafures of one of the richeft dominions of the earth. " Defpicable victories !" exclaimed Montagne, on recollecting the vile object of thefe conquefts. " Never did ambition (adds he) never did public animofities, urge mankind to perfecute each other with fuch horrible hoftilities, or fuch deplorable calamities."

Thus did the Peruvians become the woeful victims of an avaricious people, who at firft gave no figns but thofe of peace and even friendfhip. An ignorance of our vices, and the fimplicity of their own manners, threw them into the arms of a bafe enemy. In vain had immenfe tracts of land and water feparated the cities of the fun from our world, for they became our prey, and even the moft precious part of our dominions. What a fight to the Spaniards were the gardens of the temple of the fun ! where the trees, fruits, and flowers were of folid gold, and worked with an art unknown to Europeans. The walls of the temple itfelf lined with the fame metal : an infinite number of ftatues covered with precious ftones, and an immenfe quantity of other treafures, till then unknown, dazzled the conquerors of that unhappy people, and made them forget, in the midft of their cruelties, that the Peruvians were men. An analyfis of the manners of thefe unfortunate people, equally concife

with

with that we have here given of their calamities, shall finish that introduction which was thought neceffary to the fubfe-quent Letters.

The Peruvians were in general of an ingenuous and hu-mane difpofition; the attachment which they had to their religion, made them rigid obfervers of the laws; for they regarded them as the work of Mancecapac, the fon of that luminary which they adored. Though the Sun was the only god to whom they erected temples, yet they acknow-ledged, as fuperior to him, a God the Creator, whom they called *Pachacamac*; and this was, with them, the fu-preme appellation, was rarely pronounced, and always ac-companied with figns of the moft awful admiration. They had moreover a great veneration for the moon, which they regarded as the wife and fifter of the fun. They confidered her alfo as the mother of all things; but they believed, as do all the Indians, that fhe would caufe the diffolution of the world, by falling upon the the earth, and thereby deftroying it. The thunder, which they called Yalpor, and the lightning, paffed among them as minifters of juftice to the Sun; and this idea contributed not a little to in-fpire them with that awful refpect they had for the firft Spaniards, whofe fire-arms they took to be the inftru-ments of thunder.

The

The opinion of the immortality of the foul was established among the Peruvians. They suppofed, as do the greateft part of the Indians, that the foul went into fome unknown region, where it was rewarded or punifhed according to its merit.

Gold, and all that was the moft precious among them, compofed the offerings which they made to the Sun. The *Raymi* was the principal feaft of that god, to whom they prefented a cup of *mays*, a kind of ftrong liquor, which they were fkilful in extracting from one of their plants, and of which they drank, even to intoxication, after their facrifices. To the temple of the Sun there were a hundred doors. The reigning Inca, whom they called Capa Inca, had the fole right of opening thefe doors : and alfo to him alone belonged the right of penetrating into the interior parts of the temple. The virgins, who were devoted to the Sun, were there educated, almoft from their birth ; and they there preferved a perpetual virginity, under the conduct of their mamas, or governors ; unlefs when the law had ordained any of them to efpoufe the Inca, who was always to marry his fifter, or when he had no fifter, the firft princefs of the blood, who was a virgin of the Sun. One of the principal occupations of thefe virgins was to prepare the diadems for the Incas, of which a fort of fringe compofed the only ornament. This temple was decorated

with

with the different idols of nations who had submitted to the Incas, after they had been made to embrace the worship of the Sun. The richness of the metals, and of the precious stones with which it was embellished, gave it a magnificence and splendour worthy of that divinity to whom it was confecrated. The obedience and reverence of the Peruvians for their king was founded on the belief that the Sun was the father of their monarchs ; but their fidelity and affection for them was the fruit of the virtue and equitable government of the Incas themselves. The youths of the country were educated with all that care which the happy simplicity of their morals inspired. Subordination was there submitted to with alacrity, because they were early accustomed to it, and tyranny and pride had there no place. Modesty and mutual affection were the first principles of their education. Careful to correct each error in its infancy, they who had the charge of their youth, either suppressed a rising passion, or turned it to the advantage of society. There are some virtues which necessarily include many others. To give an idea of those of the Peruvians, it is sufficient to say, that before the defcent of the Spaniards, it passes for an indisputable fact, that no Peruvian was ever known to utter a falsity.

The *Amautas*, or philosophers of that nation, taught their youths the discoveries they had made in the sciences. The Peruvians were yet in the infancy of that fort of know-

ledge :

large : they were, however, in the full vigour of happinefs. This people had lefs information, lefs knowledge, fewer arts, than we have; and yet they had fufficient to provide them with every neceffary of life. The quapas or quipos* ferving them inftead of our writing. Strings of cotton or of guts, with which other ftrings of different colours were united, reminded them, by means of knots placed at certain diftances, of things they defired to remember. By the help of thefe they preferved their annals, their codes, their rituals, &c. They had alfo public officers whom they called *Quipocamaios*, to the care of whom their quipos were committed. The finances, the difburfements, the tributes, all matters, all combinations, were as eafily regulated by quipos, as they could have been by writing. The fage legiflator of Peru, Mancocapac, had inftituted the culture of the earth as a facred right; they enjoyed their lands in common, and the days of their labour were the days of feftivity. Canals, of a prodigious extent, diftributed every where refrefhment and fertility; and, what is fcarce credible, without any inftrument of iron or fteel, but by the mere force of labour, thefe people were able to overthrow rocks, and cut through the higheft mountains, in order to carry their ftupendous aqueducts, or their public roads, through every part of their dominions. The Peruvians knew as much of geometry as was neceffary to meafure

---

* The quipos of Peru were alfo in ufe with many other nations of South America.

and divide their lands.   Physic was there unknown as a science, though they had fome medical fecrets which were practifed on particular occafions.   Garcilaffo reports, that they had a fort of mufic, and even fome kinds of poetry. Their poets, whom they called *Hafavec*, compofed a fpecies of tragedy and comedy, which the fons of the caciques*, or the curaccas† reprefented, during their feftival times, before the incas and the court.   Morality, and the knowledge of the laws neceffary to the welfare of fociety, were therefore the only fciences in which the Peruvians appear to have been well fkilled.   " It muft be allowed (fays an hiftorian‡) that they have made fuch great advances in the fcience of policy, and have eftablifhed fo folid an economy, that there will be found but few nations who can boaft of having excelled them in thefe matters."

* The caciques were a fort of governors of provinces.

† Sovereigns of a fmall territory.   Thefe never appeared before the incas and the queens, without offering them a tribute of the curiofities which the province where they commanded produced.

‡ Puffendorf.   Introduction to Hiftory.

PERUVIAN PRINCESS, Lett.I.p.13.

Zilia, forced from the Temple of
the Sun, by the Spanish Soldiers.

LETTERS

OF A

PERUVIAN PRINCESS.

LETTER I.

To Aza : account of her being taken out of the temple of the Sun by the Spaniards.

AZA! my dear Aza! the cries of thy tender Zilia, like a morning vapour, exhale and are diffipated before they arrive in thy prefence : in vain I call thee to my fuccour; in vain I expect thy love to come, and break the chains of my flavery; alas! perhaps the misfortunes I am yet ignorant of are the moft terrible! perhaps thy woes furpafs even mine! The city of the Sun, delivered to the fury of a barbarous nation, fhould make my eyes overflow with tears; but my grief, my fears, my defpair, are for thee alone

Dear foul of my life, what wert thou doing in that frightful tumult? Was thy courage fatal or ufelefs to thee? Cruel alternative! diſtracting anxiety! O my dear Aza, mayeſt thou yet live in fafety, and may I fink, if it be needful, under the ills that opprefs me. Since the terrible moment (which fhould have been fnatched out of the chain of time, and replunged into the eternal ideas) fince the moment of horror wherein thefe impious favages bore me away from the worfhip of the fun, from myfelf, from my love; retained in clofe captivity, deprived of all communication, ignorant of the language of thefe fierce men; I experience only the effects of misfortune, without being able to difcover the caufe of it. Plunged in an abyfs of obfcurity, my days refemble the moft dreadful nights,

nights. Far from being affected with my complaints, my ravishers are not touched even with my tears; equally deaf to my language and to the cries of my despair. What people are there so savage as to be unmoved at the signs of anguish? What dreary desert could produce human beings insensible to the voice of groaning Nature? O the barbarians, savage masters of the thunder*, and of the power to exterminate; cruelty is the sole guide of their actions. Aza, how wilt thou escape their fury? Where art thou? In what situation? If my life is dear to thee, inform me of thy destiny.

Alas! how is mine changed. Whence can it be, that days, in themselves so like one another, should, with respect to me, have such fatal differences? Time rolls on, dark succeeds light, nothing in nature appears out of order; but I, of late supremely happy, lo, I am fallen into the horror of despair! nor was there an interval to prepare me for this fearful change. Thou knowest, O delight of my heart, that on that terrible day, that day for ever dreadful, the triumph of our union was to have shone forth. Scarce did it begin to appear, when impatient to execute a project which my tenderness had inspired me with in the night, I ran to my quipos†, and, taking advantage of the silence which then reigned in the temple, hastened to knot them, in hopes that by their assistance I might render immortal the history of our love and our felicity. As I proceeded in my work, the undertaking appeared to me less difficult: the clue of innumerable threads by degrees grew under my fingers a faithful painting of our actions and our sentiments; as it was heretofore the interpreter of our thoughts

---

* Alluding to the cannon.

† A great number of strings of different colours, which the Indians use for want of writing, in accounting the pay of their troops and the number of their people. Some authors pretend that they made use of them also to transmit to posterity the memorable actions of their Incas.

during

during the long intervals of our abfence from each
other. Wholly taken up with my employment, I
forgot how time paffed, when a confufed noife awakened my fpirits, and put my heart in a flutter. I
thought the happy moment was arrived, and that the
hundred gates* were opening to give a free paffage to
the fun of my days: precipitately I hid my quipos
under the lappet of my robe, and ran to meet thee.
But how horrible was the fpectacle that appeared before my eyes! The frightful idea of it will never be
effaced out of my memory.

The pavement of the temple ftained with blood;
the image of the fun trodden under foot; our affrighted
virgins flying before a troop of furious foldiers, who
maffacred all that oppofed their paffage; our mamas†
expiring under their wounds, their garments ftill
burning with the fire of their thunder; the groans of
difmay, the cries of rage, fpreading dread and horror
on every fide, brought me at laft to a fenfe of my mifery. Being returned to myfelf, I found that by a
natural, and almoft involuntary motion, I was got
behind the altar, which I embraced. There I faw
the barbarians pafs by: I did not dare to give free
paffage to my panting breath, for fear it fhould coft
me my life. I remarked, however, that the effect of
their cruelty abated at the fight of the precious ornaments that overfpread the temple; that they feized
thofe whofe luftre ftruck them moft fenfibly; and that
they even plucked off the plates of gold that lined the
walls. I judged that theft was the motive of their
barbarity, and that, to avoid death, my only way
was to conceal myfelf from their fight. I defigned to
have got out of the temple, to have been conducted to
thy palace, to have demanded fuccour of the Capa
Inca‡, and an afylum for my companions and me:

* In the temple of the Sun were a hundred gates, which
the Inca only had power to have opened. -
† A kind of governance over the virgins of the Sun.
‡ The general name of the reigning Inca.

but

but no fooner did I attempt to ftir, than I was arrefted. Oh my dear Aza! then did I tremble! thefe impious men dared to lay their hands upon the daughter of the Sun.

Torn from the facred abode, dragged ignominioufly out of the temple, I faw, for the firft time, the threfhold of the celeftial gate, which I ought not to have paffed but with the enfigns of royalty*. Inftead of the flowers which fhould have been ftrewed under my feet, I faw the ways covered with blood and carnage : inftead of the honours of the throne, which I was to have partaken of with thee, I find myfelf a flave under the laws of tyranny, fhut up in an obfcure prifon, the place that I occupy in the univerfe is bounded by the extent of my being. A mat, bathed with tears, receives my body, fatigued by the torments of my foul : But, dear fupport of my life, how light will all thefe evils be to me, if I can but learn that thou yet breathest.

In the midft of this horrible defolation, I know not by what happy chance I have preferved my qui-pos. I have them in poffeffion, my dear Aza ; they are the treafure of my heart, as they ferve to inter-pret both thy love and mine ; the fame knots which fhall inform thee of my exiftence, changing their form under thy hands, will inftruct me alfo in thy deftiny. Alas! by what way fhall I convey them to thee ? By what addrefs can they be reftored to me again ? I am ignorant at prefent : but the fame underftanding which taught us their ufe, will fuggeft to us the means to deceive our tyrants. Whoever the faithful chaqui† may be that fhall bring thee this precious depofit, I fhall envy his happinefs. He will fee thee, my dear Aza, and I would give all the days allotted me by the fun to enjoy thy prefence one moment,

* The virgins confecrated to the Sun entered the temple almoft as foon as born, and never came out till the day of their marriage.

† Meffenger.

LETTER

LETTER II.

To AZA : *history of the first sight of, and engagement to him.*

MAY the tree of virtue, my dear Aza, for ever spread its shadow over the pious citizen who received under my window the mysterious tissue of my thoughts, and delivered it into thy hands. May Pachacamac* prolong his years, as the recompense of his address in conveying to me divine pleasures with thy answer. The treasures of love are open to me; I draw from thence a delicious joy that inebriates my soul. While I unravel the secrets of thy heart, my own bathes itself in a sea of perfumes. Thou livest, and the chains that were to unite us are not broken. So much felicity was the object 'of my desires, but not of my hopes.

Whilst I abandoned all thought of myself, my fears for thee deprived me of all pleasure. Thou restorest to me all that I had lost. I taste deep draughts of the sweet satisfaction of pleasing thee, of being praised by thee, of being approved by him I love. But, dear Aza, while I swim in these delights, I do not forget that I owe to thee what I am. As the rose draws his brilliant colours from the rays of the sun, so the charms which please thee in my spirit and sentiments are the benefits of thy luminous genius; nothing is mine, but my tenderness. If thou hadst been an ordinary man, I had remained in that ignorance to which my sex is condemned; but thou, not the slave of custom, hast broken the barrier, in order to elevate me to thyself. Thou didst not suffer a being like thy own to be confined to the humble advantage of only giving life to thy posterity; it was thy pleasure that our Amutas† should adorn my under-

---

* The creator God, more powerful than the Sun.

† Indian philosophers.

C   standing

standing with their sublime intelligences. But O, light of my life, could I have resolved to abandon my tranquil ignorance, and engage in the painful occupation of study, had it not been with the desire of pleasing thee? Without a desire to merit thy esteem, thy confidence, thy respect, by virtues that fortify love, and which love renders voluptuous, I had been only the object of thy eyes; absence would already have effaced thee out of my memory.

But, alas! if thou lovest me still, why am I in slavery? Casting a look upon the walls of my prison, my joy disappears, horror seizes me, and my fears are renewed. They have not robbed thee of liberty, yet thou comest not to my succour: Thou hast been informed of my situation, and it is not changed. No, my dear Aza, among these savage people, whom thou callest Spaniards, thou art not so free as thou imaginest thyself. I behold as many signs of slavery in the honours which they render thee, as in my own captivity. Thy goodness seduces thee; thou thinkest the promises, which those barbarians make thee by their interpreters, sincere, because thy own words are inviolable; but I, who understand not their language, whom they think not worthy to be deceived, behold their actions. Thy subjects take them for gods, and join their party. O my dear Aza, wretched the people who are determined by fear! Extricate thyself from thy error, and suspect the false goodness of these foreigners. Abandon thy empire, since the Inca Viracocha* had predicted its destruction. Redeem thy life and thy liberty at the price of thy power, thy grandeur, and thy treasures: the gifts of nature alone will then remain to thee, and our days shall pass in safety. Rich in the possession of our hearts, great by our virtues, powerful by our mo-

---

* Viracocha was looked upon as a god, and the Indians firmly believe that at his death he predicted that the Spaniards should dethrone one of his descendants.

deration,

deration, we fhall, in a cottage, enjoy the heaven, the
earth, and our mutual tendernefs. Thou wilt be
more a king in reigning over my foul, than in doubting of the affection of a people without number : my
fubmiffion to thy will fhall caufe thee to enjoy, without tyranny, the undifputed right of commanding.
While I obey thee, I will make thy empire refound
with my joyous fongs ; thy diadem* fhall be always
the work of my hands, and thou fhalt lofe nothing of
royalty but the cares and fatigues.

How often, dear foul of my life, haft thou com-
plained of the duties of thy rank ? How have the ceremonies, which accompanied thy vifits, made thee
envy the lot of thy fubjects? Thy wifh was to live
for me only. Art thou now afraid to lofe fo many
conftraints ? Shall I be no more that Zilia, whom
thou preferredft to thy empire ? I cannot entertain
the thought : my heart is not changed, and why fhould
there be a change in thine ?

I love : the fame Aza who reigned in my heart the
firft moment I faw him, is for ever before me : continually do my thoughts recal that happy day, when
thy father, my fovereign lord, gave thee, for the firft
time, a fhare of that power referved for him only, of
entering the inner part of the temple†. Fancy ftill
figures to me the agreeable fpectacle of our virgins,
who, being there affembled, received a new luftre
from the admirable order that reigns among them :
fo in a garden we fee the arrangement of the fineft
flowers adds a brilliancy to their beauty. Thou ap-
pearedft in the midft of us like a rifing fun, whofe
tender light prepares the ferenity of a fine day : the
fire of thy eyes overfpread our cheeks with the blufhes
of modefty, and our looks were held captive in fweet
confufion : thy eyes, at the fame time, fhot forth a

* The diadem of the Incas was a kind of fringe, wrought by
the virgins of the Sun.

† The reigning Inca alone has a right to enter into the
temple of the Sun.

C 2   brilliant

brilliant joy ; for never before had they met fo many beauties together. The Capa-Inca was the only man we had till then feen. Aftonifhment and filence reigned on every fide. I know not what were the thoughts of my companions : but the fentiments that attacked my own heart, who can exprefs ? For the firft time I had the united fenfe of trouble, inquietude, and plea-fure. Confufed with the agitations of my foul, I was going to hide myfelf from thy fight : but thou turnedft thy fteps towards me, and I was retained by refpect. O my dear Aza, the remembrance of this firft moment of my happinefs will be always dear to me. The found of thy voice, like the melodious chanting of our hymns, conveyed into my veins that foft tremor, and holy refpect, which is infpired by the prefence of the divinity.

Trembling, difmayed, my timidity had taken from me even the ufe of my fpeech : but, emboldened at laft by the foftnefs of thy words, I dared to lift up my looks towards thee, and met thine. No, death itfelf fhall never efface from my memory the tender move-ments of our fouls at this meeting, and how in an in-ftant they were blended together. If we could doubt of our original, my dear Aza, this glance of light would have deftroyed our uncertainty. What other principle, but that of fire could have tranfmitted be-twixt us this lively intelligence of hearts, which was communicated, fpread, and felt with an inexplicable rapidity ? I was too ignorant of the effects of love, not to be deceived by it. With an imagination full of the fublime theology of our cucipatas*, I took the fire which animated me for a divine agitation ; I thought the Sun had manifefted to me his will by thee his organ, that he chofe me for his felected fpoufe ! I fighed in rapture :---but after thy departure, ex-amining my heart, I found there nothing but thy image.

* Priefts of the Sun.

What

What a change, my dear Aza, did thy prefence make in me! All objects appeared to me new, and it feemed as if I now faw my fellow virgins the firft time. How did their beauty brighten! I could not bear their prefence, but, retiring afide, gave way to the anxiety of my foul, when one of them came to waken me out of my reverie, by giving me frefh matter to heighten it: fhe informed me, that, being thy neareft relation, I was deftined to be thy wife, as foon as my age would permit that union. I was ignorant of the laws of thy empire*; but, after I had feen thee, my heart was too much enlightened not to have the idea of happinefs in an union with thee. Far, however, from knowing the whole extent of this union, and accuftomed to the facred name of Spoufe of the Sun, my hopes were bounded to the feeing of thee daily, the adoring of thee, and offering my vows to thee, as to that divinity. Thou, my amiable Aza, thou thyfelf filledft up the meafure of my delight, by informing me that the auguft rank of thy wife would affociate me to thy heart, to thy throne, to thy glory, to thy virtues; that I fhould inceffantly enjoy thofe fo precious converfations, thofe converfations fo fhort in proportion to our defires, which would adorn my mind with the perfections of thy foul, and add to my felicity the delicious hope of being hereafter a happinefs to thee. O my dear Aza, how flattering to my heart was that impatience of thine, fo often exprefled on account of my youth, which retarded our union! How long did the courfe of two years appear to thee, and yet how fhort was their duration! Alas! the fortunate moment was arrived! What fatality rendered it woeful? What God was it who punifhed innocence and virtue in this manner? or,

---

* The laws of the Indians obliged the Incas to marry their fifters; and when they had none, to take the firft princefs of the blood of the Incas that was a virgin of the Sun.

what

what infernal power feparated us from ourfelves?
Horror feizes me,---my heart is rent,---my tears bedew my work.   Aza! my dear Aza!

LETTER III.

*To Aza : her being put on fhip-board, ficknefs, and cap-
ture by the French.*

IT is thou, dear light of my foul, it is thou who
calleft me back to life.   Would I preserve it, if I was
not fure that death, by a fingle ftroke, would mow
down thy days and mine? I touched the moment in
which the fpark of divine fire, wherewith the fun
animates our being, was going to expire.   Laborious
nature was already preparing to give another form to
that portion of matter which belonged to her in me:
I was dying; thou waft lofing for ever half of thyfelf, when my love reftored my life, which I now facrifice to thee.   But how can I inform thee of the
furprifing things that have happened to me? How fhall
I call back ideas that were confufed even when I received them, and which the time that is fince paffed
renders ftill lefs intelligible?
   Scarcely, my dear Aza, had I entrufted our faithful
chaqui with the laft tiffue of my thoughts, when I
heard a great motion in our habitation: about mid-
night two of my ravifhers came to hurry me out of
my gloomy retreat, with as much violence as they had
employed in fnatching me from the temple of the Sun.
Though the night was very dark, they made me travel
fo far, that, finking under the fatigue, they were
obliged to carry me into a houfe, which I could perceive, notwithftanding the obfcurity, it was exceedingly
difficult to get into.   I was thruft into a place more
ftrait and inconvenient than my prifon had been.   Ah,
my dear Aza! could I perfuade thee of what I do

not

not comprehend myfelf, if thou wert not affured that a lie never fullied the lips of a child of the Sun*?

This houfe, which I judged to be very great by the quantity of people it contained, was not fixed to the ground, but being, as it were, fufpended, kept in a continual balancing motion. O light of my mind, Ticalviracocha fhould have filled my foul, like thine, with his divine fcience, to have enabled me to comprehend this prodigy. All that I know of it is, that this dwelling was not built by a being friendly to mankind: for fome moments after I had entered it, the continual motion of it, joined to a noxious fmell, made me fo violently ill, that I am furprifed I did not die of the malady. This was the beginning only of my pains.

A pretty long time paffed, and I had no confiderable fuffering, when one morning I was frighted out of my fleep by a noife more hideous than that of Yalpa. Our habitation received fuch fhocks as the earth will experience, when the moon, by her fall, fhall reduce the univerfe to duft†. The cries of human voices, joined to this wild uproar, rendered it ftill more frightful. My fenfes, feized with a fecret horror, conveyed to my foul nothing but the idea of deftruction, not of myfelf only, but of all nature. I thought the peril univerfal; I trembled for thy life: my dread grew at laft to the utmoft excefs, when I faw a company of men in fury, with bloody countenances and clothes, rufh tumultuoufly into my chamber. I could not fupport the terrible fpectacle; my ftrength and underftanding left me: ftill am I ignorant of the confequence of this terrible event. But when I recovered, I found myfelf in a pretty handfome bed, furrounded by feveral favages, who were not, however, any of the cruel Spaniards.

* It paffes for certain that no Peruvian ever lied.
† The Indians believe that the end of the world will be brought about by the fall of the moon upon the earth.

Canft

Canſt thou imagine to thyſelf my ſurprife, when I found myſelf in a new dwelling, among new men, without being able to comprehend how this change could be brought about? I ſhut my eyes, the better to recollect myſelf, and be aſſured whether I was alive, or whether my ſoul had not quitted my body to paſs into unknown regions*. I confeſs to thee, dear idol of my heart, that, fatigued with an odious life, diſ-heartened at ſuffering torments of every kind, preſſed down under the weight of my horrible deſtiny, I re-garded with indifference the end of my being, which I felt approaching: I conſtantly refuſed all the ſuſ-tenance that was offered me, and in a few days was on the verge of the fatal term, which I beheld without regret. The decay of my ſtrength annihilated my ſentiments: already my enfeebled imagination received no images but like thoſe of a ſlight deſign traced by a trembling hand; already the objects which had moſt affected me, excited in me that vague ſenſation which we feel when we indulge in an indeterminate reverie: almoſt I was no more. This fate, my dear Aza, is not ſo uneaſy as it is thought. At a diſtance it frightens us, becauſe we think of it with all our powers: when it is arrived, enfeebled by the grada-tions of pain which conduct us to it, the deciſive mo-ment appears only as the moment of repoſe. A natural propenſity which carries us towards futurity, even that futurity which will never exiſt for us, reanimated my ſpirit, and tranſported it into thy palace. I thought I arrived there at the inſtant when thou hadſt received the news of my death. I repreſented to myſelf thy pale disfigured image, ſuch as lily appears when ſcorched by the burning heat of noon. Is the moſt tender love then ſometimes barbarous? I rejoiced at thy grief, and excited it by ſorrowful adieus. I found a ſweet-neſs, perhaps a pleaſure, in diffuſing the poiſon of re-

* The Indians believe that the ſoul, after death, goes into unknown places, to be there recompenſed or puniſhed accord-ing to its deferts.

gret

gret over thy days; and the fame love which rendered
me cruel, tore my heart by the horror of thy pains.
At laft, awakened as from a profound fleep, penetrated
with thy agony, trembling for thy life, I called for
help, and again beheld the light.

Shall I fee thee again, thou, the dear arbiter of my
exiftence? Alas! who can affure me of it. I know
not where I am: perhaps it is far diftant from thee!
But fhould we be feparated by the immenfe fpaces
inhabited by the children of the Sun, the light cloud
of my thoughts fhall hover inceffantly about thee.

LETTER IV.

To AZA : *account of her treatment during her ficknefs.*

WHATEVER the love of life be, my dear Aza,
pains diminifh, defpair extinguifhes it. The contempt in which nature feems to hold our being, by
abandoning it to defpair, fhocks us·at firft: afterwards, the impoffibility of working our deliverance
proves fuch a humbling circumftance, that it leads
us to a difguft of ourfelves. I live no longer in,
nor for, myfelf: every inftant in which I breathe, is
a facrifice which I make to thy love, and from day to
day it becomes more painful. If time bring fome fo-
lace to the ills that confume me, far from clearing up
my prefent condition, it feems to render it more obfcure. All that furrounds me is unknown, all is new,
all engages my curiofity, and nothing can fatisfy it.
In vain I employ my attention and efforts to underftand or be underftood; both are equally impoffible to
me. Wearied with fo many fruitlefs pains, I thought
to dry up the fource of them, by depriving my eyes
of the impreffions they receive from objects. I per-
fifted for fome time in keeping them fhut: but the
voluntary darknefs, to which I condemned myfelf,
ferved only to relieve my modefty: offended continually at the prefence of thefe men, whofe officious kindneffes are fo many torments, my foul was not the lefs
agitated:

agitated: shut up in myself, my inquietudes were not the less sharp, and the desire to express them was the more violent. On the other hand, the impossibility of making myself understood, spread an anguish over my organs, which is not less insupportable than the pains which a more apparent reality would cause. How cruel is this situation! Alas! I thought I had begun to understand some words of the savage Spaniards; I found some agreement with our august language; I flattered myself that in a short time I should come to explain myself with them. Far from finding the same advantage among my new tyrants, they express themselves with so much rapidity that I cannot even distinguish the inflexions of their voice. All circumstances make me judge that they are not of the same nation; and by the difference of their manners and apparent character, one easily divines that Pachacamac has distributed to them in great disproportion the elements of which he formed human kind. The grave and fierce air of the first shews that they are composed of the same matter as the hardest metals. These seem to have slipped out of the hands of the creator the moment he he had collected together only air and fire for their formation. The scornful eyes, the gloomy and tranquil mien of the former, shewed sufficiently that they were cruel in cold blood; which the inhumanity of their actions has too well proved. The smiling countenance of the latter, the sweetness of their looks, a certain haste in all their actions, which seems to be a haste of good-will, prevents me in their favour, but I remark contradictions in their conduct which suspends my judgment. Two of these savages seldom quit the sides of my bed: one, which I guess to be the cacique* by his air of grandeur, seems to shew me, in his way, a great deal of respect; the other gives me part of the assistance which my malady requires; but his goodness is severe, his succours are cruel, and his familiarity imperious.

* Cacique is a kind of governor of a province.

The

The moment when, recovered from my fit, I found myself in their power, this latter (for I have obferved him well) more bold than the reft, would take me by the hand, which I drew away with inexpeffible confufion. He feemed to be furprifed at my refiftance, and without any regard to my modefty, took hold of it again immediately. Feeble, dying, and fpeaking only fuch words as were not underftood, could I hinder him? He held it, my dear Aza, as long as he thought proper; and fince that time, I am obliged to give it him myfelf feveral times every day, in order to avoid fuch difputes as always turn to my difadvantage. This kind of ceremony* feems to me a fuperftition of the people : they imagine they find fomething there which indicates the nature of a diftemper; but it muft doubtlefs be their own nation that feels the effects of it; for I perceive none; I fuffer continually by an inward fire that confumes me, and have fcarce ftrength enough left to knot my quipos. In this occupation I employ as much time as my weaknefs will permit me : the knots which ftrike my fenfes, feem to give more reality to my thoughts; the kind of refemblance which I imagine they have with words, caufes an illufion which deceives my pain : I think I fpeak to thee, tell thee of my love, affure thee of my vows and my tendernefs : the fweet error is my fupport, and my life. If the excefs of my burthen obliges me to interrupt my work, I groan at thy abfence. Given up thus entirely to my tendernefs, there is not one of my moments which belongs not to thee.

Alas! what other ufe can I make of them? O my dear Aza! if thou wert not the mafter of my foul; if the chains of love did not bind me infeparably to to thee; plunged in an abyfs of obfcurity, could I turn my thoughts away from the light of my life? Thou art the fun of my days; thou enlighteneft

* The Indians have no knowledge of phyfic.

them;

them; thou prolongeſt them, and they are thine. Thou cheriſheſt me, and I ſuffer myſelf to live. What wilt thou do for me? Thou loveſt me, and I have my reward.

LETTER V.

To Aza : ſhe deſcribes the behaviour of the French captain and his crew.

WHAT have I ſuffered, my dear Aza, ſince I conſecrated to thee my laſt knots! The loſs of my quipos was yet wanting to complete my pains: but when my officious perſecutors perceived that work to augment my diſorder, they deprived me of the uſe of them.

At laſt they have reſtored to me the treaſure of my tenderneſs; but with many tears did I purchaſe it. Only this expreſſion of my ſentiments had I remaining, the mere ſorrowful conſolation of painting my grief to thee: and could I loſe it, and not deſpair? My ſtrange deſtiny has ſnatched from me even the relief which the unhappy find in ſpeaking of their pains. One is apt to think there is pity when one is heard, and from the participation of ſorrow ariſes ſome comfort: I cannot make myſelf underſtood, and am ſurrounded with gaiety. I cannot even enjoy that new kind of entertainment to which the inability of communicating my thoughts reduces me. Environed with importunate perſons, whoſe attentive looks diſturb the compoſed ſolicitude of my ſoul, I forget the faireſt preſent which nature has made us, the power to render our ideas impenetrable without the concurrence of our will. I am ſometimes afraid that theſe curious ſavages diſcover the diſadvantageous reflections with which I am inſpired by the oddneſs of their conduct.

One moment deſtroys the opinion which another had given me of their character: for if I am ſwayed by the frequent oppoſition of their wills to mine, I cannot

not doubt but they believe me their flave, and that
their power is tyrannical. Not to reckon up an infinite number of other contradictions, they refute me,
my dear Aza, even the neceffary aliments for the fuftenance of life, and the liberty of choofing what place
I would lie in : they keep me, by a kind of violence,
in the bed, which is become infupportable to me. On
the other fide, if I reflect on the extreme concern they
have fhewn for the prefervation of my days, and the
refpect with which the fervices they render me are accompanied, I am tempted to believe that they take me
for a fpecies fuperior to human kind. Not one of
them appears before me without bending his body,
more or lefs, as. we ufed to do in worfhipping the
Sun. The Cacique feems to attempt to imitate the
ceremonial of the Incas on the days of Raymi * : he
kneels down very nigh my bed fide, and continues a
confiderable time in that painful pofture : fometimes
he keeps filent, and, with his eyes caft down, feems
to think profoundly : I fee in his countenance that
refpectful confufion which the great name† infpires us
with when fpoken aloud. If he finds an opportunity
of taking hold of my hand, he puts his mouth to it
with the fame veneration that we have for the facred
diadem‡. Sometimes he utters a great number of
words, which are not at all like the ordinary language
of his nation : the found of them is more foft, more
diftinct, and more harmonious. He joins to this that
air of concern which is the forerunner of tears, thofe
fighs which exprefs the neceffities of the foul, the moft
plaintive action, and all that ufually accompanies the
defire of obtaining favour. Alas! my dear Aza, if

* The Raymi was the principal feaft of the Sun, when the
Incas and priefts adored him on their knees.
† The great name was Pachacamac, which they fpoke but
feldom, and always with great figns of adoration.
‡ They killed the diadem of Manco Capac in the fame man-
ner as the Roman Catholics kifs the relics of their faints.

D　　　　　　　　　　　　　　h-he knew me well, if he was not in some error with regard to my being, what prayer could he have to address to me ?

Must they not be an idolatrous nation ? I have not yet seen any adoration paid by them to the Sun : perhaps they make women the object of their worship. Before the great Mancocapac* brought down to earth the will of the Sun, our ancestors deified whatever struck them with dread or pleasure ; perhaps these savages feel these two sentiments with regard to women. But if they adore me, would they add to my misfortunes the hideous constraint in which they keep me ? No ; they would endeavour to please me ; they would obey the tokens of my will : I should be free, and released from this odious habitation : I should go in search of the master of my soul, one of whose looks would efface the memory of all these misfortunes.

LETTER VI.

To AZA : *she discovers where she is ; her despair on the occasion.*

WHAT an horrible surprise, my dear Aza ! how are our woes augmented ! how deplorable is our condition ! our evils are without remedy : I have only to tell thee of them and to die. At last they have permitted me to get up, and with haste I availed myself of the liberty. I drew myself to a small window, which I opened with all the precipitation that my curiosity inspired.----What did I see ? Dear love of my life, I shall not find expressions to paint the excess of my astonishment, and the incurable despair that seized me, when I discovered round me nothing but that terrible element, the very sight of which makes me

---

* The first Legislator of the Indians. *See the History of the* Incas.

tremble.

tremble. My firſt glance did but too well inform me what occaſioned the troubleſome motion of our dwelling. I am in one of thoſe floating houſes which the Spaniards made uſe of to arrive at our unhappy country, and of which a very imperfect deſcription had been given me. Conceive, my dear Aza, what diſmal ideas entered my ſoul with this fatal knowledge. I am certain that they are carrying me from thee: I breathe no more the ſame air, nor do I inhabit the ſame element. Thou wilt ever be ignorant where I am, whether I love thee, whether I exiſt; even the diſſolution of my being will not appear an event conſiderable enough to be conveyed to thee. Dear arbiter of my days, of what value will my life be to thee hereafter? Permit me to render to the divinity an inſupportable benefit, which I can no more enjoy: I ſhall not ſee thee again, and I will live no longer. In loſing what I love, the univerſe is annihilated to me: it is now nothing but a vaſt deſert, which I fill with the cries of my love. Hear them, dear object of my tenderneſs; be touched with them, and ſuffer me to die!

What error ſeduces me? my dear Aza, it is not thou that makeſt me live: it is timid nature, which ſhuddering with horror, lends this voice, more powerful than its own, to retard an end which to her is always formidable:---but it is over;---the moſt ready means ſhall deliver me from her regrets.---Let the ſea for ever ſwallow up in its waves my unhappy tenderneſs, my life, and my deſpair.---Receive, moſt unfortunate Aza, receive the laſt ſentiments of my heart, which never admitted but thy image, was willing to live but for thee, and dies full of thy love. I love thee, I think it, I feel it ſtill, and I tell it thee for the laſt time.---

LETTER

LETTER VII.

To AZA : *she repents of her desperate purpose.*

AZA, thou haft not loft all : I breathe, and thou reigneft ftill in one heart. The vigilance of thofe who watch me defeated my fatal defign, and I have only the fhame left of having attempted its execution. It would be too long to inform thee of the circumftances of an enterprife that failed as foon as it was projected, Should I have dared ever to lift up my eyes to thee, if thou hadft been a witnefs of my paffion ? My reafon, fubjected to defpair, was no longer a fuccour to me : my life feemed to me worth nothing : I had forgot thy love.

How cruel is a cool temper after fury ! how different are the points of fight on the fame object ! In the horror of defpair ferocity is taken for courage, and the fear of fuffering for firmnefs of mind. Let a look, a furprife call us back to ourfelves, and we find that weaknefs only was the principle of our heroifm ; that repentance is the fruit of it, and contempt the recompenfe. The knowledge of my fault is the moft fevere punifhment on it.----Abandoned to the bitternefs of repentance, buried under the veil of fhame, I hold myfelf at a diftance, and fear that my body occupies too much fpace : I would hide it from the light : my tears flow in abundance : my grief is calm, not a figh expires, though I am quite given up to it. Can I do too much to expiate my crime ? it was againft thee. In vain, for two days together, thefe beneficent favages have endeavoured to make me a partaker of the joy that tranfports them. I am in continual doubt what can be the caufe of this joy ; but, even if I knew it better, I fhould not think myfelf worthy to fhare in their feftivals. Their dances, their jovial exclamations, a red liquor like

mays,

mays*, of which they drink abundantly, their eagernefs to view the fun whenever they can perceive him,
would fully convince me that their rejoicings were in
honour of that divine luminary, if the conduct of the
Cacique was conformable to that of the reft.

But, far from taking part of the public joy, fince
the fault I committed, he interefts himfelf only in my
forrow. His zeal is more refpectful, his cares are
more affiduous, and his attention is more exact and
curious. He underftood that the continual prefence
of the favages of his train, about me, was an addition to my affliction; he has delivered me from their
troublefome officioufnefs, and I have now fcarcely any
but his to fupport.

Wouldft thou believe it, my dear Aza, there are
fome moments in which I feel a kind of fweetnefs in
thefe mute dialogues; the fire of his eyes recals to
my mind the image of that which I have feen in
thine: the fimilitude is fuch that it feduces my heart.
Alas, that this illufion is tranfient, and that the regrets which follow it are durable! they will end only
with my life, fince I live for thee alone.

LETTER VIII.

To Aza : *fhe is fhewn the land.*

WHEN a fingle object unites all our thoughts, my
dear Aza, we intereft ourfelves no farther in events
than as we find them affimilated to our own cafe. If
thou waft not the only mover of my foul, could I
have paffed, as I have juft done, from the horror of
defpair to the moft flattering hope? The Cacique had

* Mays is a plant whereof the Indians make a very ftrong
and falutary drink, which they offer to the Sun on fcftival days,
and get drunk with after the facrifice is over. *See Hiftory of the
Incas.* Vol II.

before, several times, in vain attempted to entice me to
that window, which I now cannot look at without
shuddering.   At last, prevailed on by fresh solicita-
tions, I suffered myself to be conducted to it.   Oh,
my dear Aza, how well was I recompensed for my
complaisance!   By an incomprehensible miracle, in
making me look through a kind of hollow cane, he
shewed me the earth at a distance; whereas, without
the help of this wonderful machine, my eyes could
not have reached it.   At the same time he made me
understand by signs, (which began to grow familiar
to me) that we were going to that land, and that
the sight of it was the only cause of those rejoicings
which I took for a sacrifice to the Sun.   I was immediately sensible of all the benefit of this discovery:
Hope, like a ray of light, glanced directly to the
bottom of my heart.

They are certainly carrying me to this land which
they have shewn me, and which is evidently a part of
thy empire, since the sun there sheds his beneficent
rays*.   I am no longer in the fetters of the cruel
Spaniards: Who then shall hinder my returning under thy laws? Yes, my dear Aza, I go to be reunited to what I love: my love, my reason, my desires, all assure me of it.   I fly into thy arms: a torrent of joy overflows my soul; the past is vanished;
my misfortunes are ended, they are forgotten: Futurity alone employs me, and is my sole good.

Aza, my dear hope, I have not lost thee; I shall see
thy countenance, thy robes, thy shadow, I shall love
thee, and tell thee of it with my own mouth: Can
any torments efface such a felicity?

* The Indians know not our hemisphere, and believe that
the sun enlights only the land of his children.

LETTER IX.

To Aza: she learns some French names, and repeats other words, without knowing their meaning.

HOW long are the days, my dear Aza, when one computes their paſſage! Time, like ſpace, is known only by its limits. Our hopes ſeem to me the hopes of time; if they quit us, or are not diſtinctly marked, we perceive no more of their duration than of the air which fills the vaſt expanſe. Ever ſince the fatal inſtant of our ſeparation, my heart and ſoul, worn with misfortune, continued ſunk in that total abſence, that oblivion which is the horror of nature, the image of nothing: The days paſſed away without my regarding them, for not a hope fixed my attention to their length. But hope now marks every inſtant of them; their duration ſeems to me infinite; and what ſurpriſes me moſt or all is, that, in recovering the tranquillity of my ſpirit, I recover at the ſame time, a facility of thinking. Since my imagination has been opened to joy, a crowd of thoughts preſent themſelves, and employ it even to fatigue: Projects of pleaſure and happineſs ſucceed one another alternately; new id as find an eaſy reception, and ſome are even imprinted without my ſearch, and before I perceive it. Within theſe two days I underſtand ſeveral words of the Cacique's language, which I was not before acquainted with. But they are only terms applicable to objects, not expreſſive of my thoughts, nor ſufficient to make me underſtand thoſe of others: They give me ſome lights, however, which were neceſſary for my ſatisfaction. I know that the name of the Cacique is Deterville; that of our floating houſe, a ſhip; and that of the country we are going to, France.

The latter at firſt frightened me, as I did not remember to have heard any province of thy kingdom
called

called fo: But reflecting on the infinite number of countries under thy dominion, the names of which I have forgot, my fear quickly vanished. Could it long fubfift with that folid confidence which the fight of the fun gives me inceffantly? No, my dear Aza, that divine luminary enlightens only his children. To doubt this would be criminal in me: I am returning into thy empire; I am on the point of feeing thee; I run to my felicity.

Amidft the tranfports of my joy, gratitude prepares me a delicious pleafure. Thou wilt load with honour and riches the beneficent Cacique, who fhall reftore us one to the other: He fhall bear into his own country the remembrance of Zilia; the recompenfe of his virtue fhall render him ftill more virtuous, and his happinefs fhall be thy glory. Nothing can compare, my dear Aza, to the kindnefs he fhews me. Far from treating me as his flave, he feems to be mine. He is now altogether as complaifant to me, as he was contradictory during my ficknefs. My perfon, my inquietudes, my amufements, feem to make up his whole employment, and to engage all his care. I admit his offices with lefs confufion, fince cuftom and reflection have informed me that I was in an error with regard to the idolatry I fufpected him guilty of. Not that he does not continue to repeat much the fame demonftrations which I took for worfhip; but the tone, the air, and manner he makes ufe of, perfuade me that it is only a diverfion, in his country manner.

He begins by making me pronounce diftinctly fome words in his language, and he knows well that the gods do not fpeak. As foon as I have repeated after him, *Oui, je vous aime,* ' Yes, I love you,' or elfe, *Je promets d'être à vous,*' I promife to be your's,' joy expands over his countenance, he kiffes my hands with tranfport, and with an air of gaiety quite contrary to that gravity which accompanies divine adoration. Eafy as I am on the head of religion, I

am

am not quite so with regard to the country from whence he comes. His language and his apparel are so different from our's, that they sometimes shock my confidence: uneasy reflections sometimes cloud over my dear hope; I pass successively from fear to joy, and from joy to inquietude. Fatigued with the confusion of my thoughts, sick of the uncertainties that torment me, I had resolved to think no more on the subject: But what can abate the anxiety of a soul deprived of all communication, that acts only on itself, and is excited to reflect by such important interests? I cannot express my impatience, my dear Aza; I search for information with an eagerness that devours me, and yet continually find myself in the most profound obscurity. I know that the privation of a sense may, in some respects deceive; and yet I see with surprise, that the use of all mine drag me on from error to error. Would the intelligence of tongues be a key to the soul? O my dear Aza, how many grievous truths do I see through my misfortunes! But far from me be these troublesome thoughts: We touch the land; the light of my days shall in a moment dissipate the darkness which surrounds me.

LETTER X.

To Aza: *her arrival in France.*

I AM at last arrived at this land, the object of my desires: but, my dear Aza, I do not yet see any thing that confers the happiness I had promised myself: every object strikes, surprises, astonishes, and leaves on me only a vague impression, and stupid perplexity, which I do not attempt to throw off. My errors destroy my judgment; I remain uncertain, and almost doubt of what I behold. Scarce were we got out of the floating-house, but we entered a town built on the

the sea-shore. The people, who followed us in crowds, appeared to be of the same nation as the Cacique: and the houses did not at all resemble those of the cities of the Sun: but if these surpass in beauty, by the richness of their ornaments, those are to be preferred, on account of the prodigies with which they are filled. Upon entering the room assigned me by Deterville, my heart leaped: I saw fronting the door, a young person dressed like a virgin of the Sun, and ran to her with open arms. How great was my surprise to find nothing but an impenetrable resistance where I saw a human figure move in a very extended space! Astonishment held me immovable, with my eyes fixed upon this object, when Deterville made me observe his own figure on the side of that which engaged all my attention: I touched him, I spoke to him, and I saw him at the same very near and very far from me. These prodigies confound reason, and blind the judgment. What ought we to think of the inhabitants of this country? should we fear, or should we love them? I will not take upon me to come to any determination upon so nice a subject. The Cacique made me understand, that the figure which I saw was my own! But what information does that give me? Does it make the wonder less great? Am I the less mortified to find nothing but error and ignorance in my mind? With grief I see it, my dear Aza; the least knowing in this country are wiser than all our Amutas.

The Cacique has given me a young and very sprightly China*, and it affords me great pleasure to see a woman again, and to be served by her. Many others of my sex wait upon me; but I had rather they would let it alone, for their presence awakens my fears. One may see by their manner of looking on me, that they had never been at Cuzco†. However,

* A maid-servant or chambermaid.
† The capital of Peru.

as

as my fpirit floats continually in a fea of uncertainties, I can judge of nothing. My heart, alone un-
fhaken, defires, expects, waits for one happinefs only,
without which all the reft is pain and vexation.

LETTER XI.

To AZA : *feveral remarks on what fhe fees.*

THOUGH I have taken all the pains in my power
to gain fome light with refpect to my prefent fituation,
I am no better informed at this inftant than I was
three days ago. All that I have been able to obferve
is, that the other favages of this country appear as
good and as humane as the Cacique. They fing and
dance, as if they had lands to cultivate every day*.
---If I was to form a judgment from the oppofition
of their cuftoms to thofe of our nation, I fhould not
have the leaft hope : but I remember that thy auguft
father fubjected to his obedience provinces very remote, the people of which had nothing in common
with us. Why may not this be one of thofe provinces ? The fun feems pleafed to enlighten it, and
his beams are more bright and pure than I ever faw
them†. This infpires me with confidence, and I
am uneafy only to think how long it muft be before
I can be fully informed of what regards our interefts :
for, my dear Aza, I am very certain that the knowledge of the language of the country will be fufficient
to teach me the truth, and allay my inquietudes. I
let flip no opportunity of learning it, and avail myfelf of all the moments wherein Deterville leaves me
at liberty, to take the inftructions of my China.---
Little fervice indeed they do me ; for, as I cannot

---

* The lands in Peru are cultivated in common, and the
days they are about this work, are always days of rejoicing.

† The fun never fhines clear in Peru.

make

make her underſtand my thoughts, we can hold no converſation, and I learn only the names of ſuch objects as ſtrike both our ſights. The ſigns of the Cacique are ſometimes more uſeful to me: cuſtom has made it a kind of language betwixt us, which ſerves us at leaſt to expreſs our wills. He conducted me yeſterday into a houſe, where, without this knowledge, I ſhould have behaved very ill. We entered ˙ into a larger and better furniſhed apartment than that which I inhabit, and a great many people were there aſſembled. The general aſtoniſhment ſhewn at my appearance diſpleaſed me, and the exceſſive laughter which ſome young women endeavoured to ſtiſle, but which burſt out again, when they caſt their eyes on me, gave me ſuch uneaſineſs of mind, that I ſhould have taken it for ſhame, if I could have found myſelf conſcious of any fault: but, finding nothing within me but a repugnance to ſtay in ſuch company, I was going to return back, when I was detained by a ſign of Deterville. I found that I ſhould commit a fault by going out, and I took great care not to deſerve the blame that was thrown on me without cauſe. As I fixed my attention, during my ſtay, upon thoſe women, I thought I diſcovered that the ſingularity of my dreſs occaſioned the ſurpriſe of ſome, and the laughter of others. I pitied their weakneſs, and endeavoured to perſuade them by my countenance, that my ſoul did not ſo much differ from their's, as my habit differed from their ornaments.

A young man, whom I ſhould have taken for a Curaca*, if he had not been dreſſed in black, came and took me by the hand with an affable air, and led me to a woman, whom, by her haughty mien, I took for the Pallas† of the country. He ſpoke ſeveral words to her, which I remember by having heard

---

* The Curacas were petty ſovereigns of a country, who had the privilege of wearing the ſame dreſs as the Incas.

† A general name of the Indian princeſſes.

Deterville

Deterville pronounce the fame a thousand times. "What a beauty!---What fine eyes!"---"Aye," answered another man, "she has the graces and the "shape of a nymph." Except the women, who said nothing, they all repeated almost the fame words: I do not yet know their signification; but surely they express agreeable ideas, for the countenance is always smiling when they are pronounced. The Cacique seems to be extremely well satisfied with what they say. He keeps close to me, or, if he steps a little from me to speak to any one, his eyes are constantly upon me, and he shews me by signs what I am to do. For my part, I observe him very attentively, as I would not offend against the customs of a people who know so little of our's. I believe, my dear Aza, I can scarcely make thee comprehend how extraordinary the manners of these savages appear to me. They have so impatient a vivacity, that words do not suffice them for expression; but they speak as much by the motion of the body as by the found of the voice. What I fee of their continual agitation, has fully convinced me how little importance there was in that behaviour of the Cacique which caused me so much uneasiness, and upon which I made so many false conjectures. Yesterday he kissed the hands of the Pallas, and of all the other women: nay, what I never saw before, he even kissed their cheeks. The men came to embrace him! some took him by the hand; others pulled him by the clothes; all with a sprightliness of which we have no idea. To judge of their minds by the vivacity of their gestures, I am sure that our measured expressions, the sublime comparisons which so naturally convey our tender sentiments and affectionate thoughts, would, to them, appear insipid. They would take our serious and modest air for stupidity, and the gravity of our gait for mere stiffness. Wouldst thou believe it, my dear Aza? if thou wert here, I could be pleased to live amongst them. A certain air of affability, spread over all they do, renders them

E   amiable;

amiable; and, if my foul was more happy, I fhould find a pleafure in the diverfity of objects that fuccefsively paffed before my eyes : but the little reference they have to thee, effaces the agreeablenefs of their novelty : thou alone art my good, and my pleafure.

LETTER XII.

To Aza : her French drefs, and account of captain Deterville's behaviour to her.

I HAVE been long, my dear Aza, without being able to beftow a moment on my favourite occupation : yet I have a great many extraordinary things to communicate to thee, and avail myfelf of this firft fhort leifure to begin my information. The next day after I had vifited the Pallas, Deterville caufed a very fine habit, of the fafhion of the country, to be brought me. After my little China had put it on, according to her fancy, fhe led me to that ingenious machine which doubles objects. Though I fhould be now habituated to its effects, I could not help being furprifed at feeing my figure ftand as if I was overagainft myfelf. My new accoutrements did not difpleafe me. Perhaps I fhould have more regretted thofe which I left off, if they had not made every body troublefome by their ftaring at me. The Cacique came into my chamber, juft as the girl was adding fome trinkets to my drefs. He ftopped at my door, and looked at me for fome time without fpeaking. So profound was his reverence, that he ftept afide to let the China go out, and inadvertently put himfelf in her place. His eyes were fixed upon me, and he examined all my perfon with fuch a ferious attention as a little difcompofed me, though I knew not the reafon of what he did. However, to fhew him my acknowledgment for his new benefactions, I offered him my hand, and, not being able to exprefs

my

my sentiments, I thought I could not say any thing more agreeable to him than some of thofe words which he amufed himself with teaching me to repeat : I endeavoured even to give them the fame tone as he did in pronunciation. What effect they inftantaneoufly had on him I know not : but his eyes fparkled, his cheeks reddened, he approached me trembling, and feemed to have a defire to fnatch me into his arms : then ftopping fuddenly he preffed my hand, and pronounced in a paffionate tone, " No---refpect---her " virtue ;" and many other words which I underftood no better than thefe. Then throwing himfelf upon his feat, on the other fide of the room, he leaned his head upon his hand, and fat moping with all the fymptoms of afflictive pain.

I was alarmed at his condition, not doubting but I had occafioned him fome uneafinefs : I drew near to him to teftify my repentance ; but he gently pufhed me away without looking at me, and I did not dare fay any thing more. I was in the greateft confufion when the fervants came in to bring us victuals : he then rofe, and we ate together, in our ufual manner, his pain feeming to have no other confequence but a little forrow : yet he was not lefs kind and good to me, which feemed to me inconceivable. I did not dare to lift up my eyes upon him, or make ufe of the figns which commonly ferved us inftead of converfation : but our meal was at a time fo different from the ufual hour of repaft, that I could not help fhewing fome tokens of furprife. All that I could underftand of his anfwer was that we were foon to change our dwelling. In effect, the Cacique, after going in and out feveral times, came and took me by the hand. I let him lead me, ftill mufing within myfelf on what had paffed, and confidering whether the change of our place was not a confequence of it. Scarce was I got without the outward door of the houfe, before he helped me up a pretty high ftep, and I advanced into

a chamber

a chamber, fo low that one could not ftand upright in it: but there was room enough for the Cacique, the China and myfelf all to fit at eafe. This little apartment is agreeably decorated, has a window on each fide that enlightens it fufficiently; but it is not fpacious enough to walk in. While I was confidering it with furprife, and endeavouring to divine what could be Deterville's reafon for fhutting us up fo clofe (O my dear Aza! how familiar prodigies are in this country) I felt this machine, or cabin, I know not what to call it, move, and change its place. This motion made me think of the floating houfe. The Cacique faw me frightened, and, as he is attentive to my leaft uneafinefs, pacified me by making me look out of one of the windows. I faw, not without extreme furprife, that this machine, fufpended pretty near the earth, moved by a fecret power which I did not comprehend. Deterville then fhewed me that feveral lamas*, of a fpecies unknown to us, went before us, and drew us after them. O light of my days! thefe people muft have a genius more than human, that enables them to invent things fo ufeful and fingular: but there muft be alfo in this nation fome great defects that moderate its power, otherwife it muft needs be miftrefs of the whole world. For four days we were fhut up in this wonderful machine, leaving it only at night to take our reft in the firft houfe we came to; and then I always quitted it with regret. I confefs, my dear Aza, that, notwithftanding my tender inquietudes, I have tafted pleafures, during this journey, that were before unknown to me. Shut up in the temple from my moft tender infancy, I was unacquainted with the beauties of the univerfe, and every thing that I fee ravifhes and enchants me. The immenfe fields, which are inceffantly changed and renewed, hurry on the attentive mind with more rapidity than we pafs over them.

* A general name for beafts.

Th

The eyes, without being fatigued, rove at once over an infinite variety of admirable objects, and at the same time are at reft. One feems to find no other bounds to the fight than thofe of the world itfelf; which error flatters us, gives us a fatisfactory idea of our own grandeur, and feems to bring us nearer to the creator of thefe wonders. At the end of a fine day, the heavens prefent us a fpectacle not lefs admirable than that of the earth. Tranfparent clouds affembled round the fun, tinctured with the moft lively colours, fhew us mountains of fhade and light in every part, and the majeftic diforder attracts our admiration till we forget ourfelves. The Cacique has had the complaifance to let me every day ftep out of the rolling cabin, in order to contemplate at leifure the wonders which he faw me admire. How delicious are the woods, my dear Aza! If the beauties of heaven and earth tranfport us far from ourfelves by an involuntary rapture, thofe of the forefts bring us back again by an inward incomprehenfible bias, the fecret of which is in nature only. When we enter thefe delightful places, an univerfal charm overflows all the fenfes, and confounds their ufe. We think we fee the cooling breeze before we feel it. The different fhades in the colours of leaves, foften the light that penetrates them, and feem to ftrike the fentiment as foon as the fight. An agreeable, but indeterminate odour leaves it difficult for us to difcern whether it affects the tafte or the fmell. Even the air, without being perceived, conveys to our bodies a pure pleafure, which feems to give us another fenfe, though it does not mark out the organ of it.

O, my dear Aza! how would thy prefence embellifh thofe pure delights! how have I defired to fhare them with thee! Wert thou the witnefs of my tender thoughts, I fhould make thee find, in the fentiments of my heart, charms more powerful than all thofe of the beauties of the univerfe.

LETTER XIII.

To Aza: she comes to Paris; Deterville's and her reception by his relations.

AT laſt, my dear Aza, I am got into a city called Paris: Our journey is at an end: but, according to all appearances, ſo are not my troubles. More attentive than ever, ſince my arrival here, to all that paſſes, my diſcoveries produce only torment, and preſage nothing but misfortunes. I find thy idea in the leaſt curious of my deſires, but cannot meet with it in any of theſe objects that I ſee. As well as I can judge by the time we ſpent in paſſing through the city, and by the great number of inhabitants with whom the ſtreets are filled, it contains more people than could be got together in two or three of our countries. I reſt on the wonders that have been told me of Quito, and could ſwear to find here ſome ſtrokes of the picture which I conceive of that great city: But alas! what a difference! This place contains bridges, rivers, trees, fields: it ſeems to be an univerſe, rather than a particular ſeat of habitation. I ſhould endeavour in vain to give thee a juſt idea of the height of the houſes. They are ſo prodigiouſly elevated, that it is more eaſy to believe nature produced them as they are, than to comprehend how men could build them.

Here it is that the family of the Cacique reſides. Their houſe is almoſt as magnificent as that of the Sun: the furniture and ſome parts of the walls are of gold, and the reſt is adorned with a various mixture of the fineſt colours, which prettily enough repreſent the beauties of nature. At my arrival, Deterville made me underſtand that he was conducting me to his mother's apartment. We found her reclined upon a bed of almoſt the ſame form with that of the Incas, and

end of the fame metal*. After having held out her
hand to the Cacique, who kiſſed it bowing almoſt to
the ground, ſhe embraced him ; but with a kindneſs
ſo cold, a joy ſo conſtrained, that, if previous information had not been given me, I ſhould not have known
the ſentiments of nature in the careſſes of this mother.
After a moment's converſation, the Cacique made me
draw near. She caſt on me a diſdainful look, and,
without anſwering what her ſon ſaid to her, continued
gravely to turn round her finger a thread, which hung
to a ſmall piece of gold.

Deterville left us, to go and meet a ſtately bulky man,
who had advanced ſome ſteps towards him. He embraced both him and a woman who was employed in the
ſame manner as the Pallas. As ſoon as the Cacique
had appeared in the chamber, a young maiden, of about
my age, ran to us, and followed him with a timid
eagerneſs that ſeemed remarkable. Joy ſhone upon
her countenance, yet did not baniſh the marks of a
ſorrow that ſeemed to affect her. Deterville embraced
her laſt, but with a tenderneſs ſo natural, that my
heart was moved at it. Alas ! my dear Aza, what
would our tranſports be, if after ſo many misfortunes,
fate ſhould reunite us ? During this time I kept near
the Pallas, whom I durſt not quit, nor look up at†,
out of reſpect. Some ſevere glances, which ſhe threw
from time to time upon me, completed my confuſion,
and put me under a conſtraint that affected my very
thoughts. At laſt, the young damſel, as if ſhe had
gueſſed at my diſorder, as ſoon as ſhe had quitted Deterville, came and took me by the hand, and led me
to a window, where we both ſat down. Though I did
not underſtand any thing ſhe ſaid to me, her eyes, full
of goodneſs, ſpoke to me the univerſal language of be-

---

* The beds, chairs, and tables of the Incas were of maſſy
gold.

† Young damſels, though of the blood royal, ſhew a profound reſpect to married women.

neficent

ificent hearts : they inspired me with a confidence
and friendship which I would willingly have expressed
to her : but not being able to utter the sentiments
of my mind, I pronounced all that I knew of her
language.

She smiled more than once, looking on Deterville
with the most tender sweetness. I was pleasing myself
with this conversation, when the Pallas spoke some
words aloud, looking sternly on my new friend ; whose
countenance immediately falling, she thrust away my
hand which she before held in her's, and took no farther
notice of me. Some time after that, an old woman,
of gloomy appearance, entered the room, went up towards the Pallas, then came and took me by the
arm, led me to a chamber at the top of the house, and
left me there alone. Though this moment could not
be esteemed the most unfortunate of my life, yet, my
dear Aza, I could not pass it without much concern.
I expected, at the end of my journey, some relief to
my fatigues, and that in the Cacique's family I should
at least meet with the same kindness as from him.
The cold reception of the Pallas, the sudden change
of behaviour in the damsel, the rudeness of this woman in forcing me from a place where I had rather
have staid, the inattention of Deterville, who did not
oppose the violence shewn me ; in a word, all circumstances that might augment the pains of an unhappy
mind, presented themselves at once with their most
rueful aspects! I thought myself abandoned by all
the world, and was bitterly deploring my dismal destiny, when I beheld my China coming in. Her presence, in my situation, seemed to me an essential good ;
I ran to her, embraced her with tears, and was more
melted when I saw her touched with my affliction.
When a mind is reduced to pity itself, the compassion
of another is very valuable. The marks of this young
woman's affection softened my anguish : I related to
her my griefs, as if she could understand me : I asked
her a thousand questions, as if it had been in her power

to anſwer them. Her tears ſpoke to my heart, and mine continued to flow, but with leſs bitterneſs than before. I thought, at leaſt, that I ſhould ſee Deterville at the hour of refreſhment; but they brought me up victuals, and I ſaw him not. Since I have loſt thee, dear idol of my heart, this Cacique is the only human creature that has ſhewn me an uninterrupted courſe of goodneſs: ſo that the cuſtom of ſeeing him became a kind of neceſſity. His abſence redoubled my ſorrow. After expecting him long in vain, I laid me down; but ſleep had not yet ſealed my eyes before I ſaw him enter my chamber, followed by the young woman whoſe briſk diſdain had ſo ſenſibly afflicted me.

She threw herſelf upon my bed, and by a thouſand careſſes ſeemed deſirous to repair the ill-treatment ſhe had given me. The Cacique ſat down by my bed-ſide, and ſeemed to receive as much pleaſure in ſeeing me again, as I enjoyed in perceiving I was not abandoned. They talked together with their eyes fixed on me, and heaped on me the moſt tender marks of affection. Inſenſibly their converſation became more ſerious. Though I did not underſtand their diſcourſe, it was eaſy for me to judge that it was founded on confidence and friendſhip. I took care not to interrupt them: but, as ſoon as they returned to my bed-ſide, I endeavoured to obtain from the Cacique ſome light with regard to thoſe particulars which had appeared to me the moſt extraordinary ſince my arrival. All that I could underſtand from his anſwer was, that the name of the young woman before me was Celina, that ſhe was his ſiſter; that the great man, whom I had ſeen in the chamber of the Pallas, was his elder brother, and the other young woman, that brother's wife. Celina became more dear to me, when I underſtood ſhe was the Cacique's ſiſter, and the company of both was ſo agreeable, that I did not perceive it was day-light before they left me. After their departure, I ſpent the reſt of the time deſtined to repoſe, in thus conversing with thee. This is my happiness, my only joy : it is to thee alone, dear soul of my thoughts, that I unbosom my heart; thou shalt ever be the sole depository of my secrets, my passions, and my sentiments.

LETTER XIV.

To AZA : she is affronted in public company.

IF I did not continue, my dear Aza, to take from my sleep the time that I give to thee, I should no more enjoy those delicious moments in which I exist for thee only. They have made me resume my virgin habits, and oblige me to remain all day in a room full of people, who are changed and renewed every moment without seeming to diminish. This involuntary dissipation, in spite of me, often causes a suspension of my tender thoughts : but if, for some moments, I lose that lively attention which unites our hearts, I find thee again in the advantageous comparisons I make of thee with whatever surrounds me. In the different countries that I have passed through, I have not seen any savages so haughtily familiar as these. The women, in particular, seem to have a kind of disdainful civility that disgusts human nature, and would perhaps inspire me with as much contempt for them as they shew for others, if I knew them better. One of them caused an affront to be given me yesterday, which still afflicts me. Just when the assembly was most numerous, after she had been speaking to several persons without perceiving me ; whether by chance, or that somebody made her take notice of me ; as soon as she cast her eyes on me, she burst out a laughing, quitted her place precipitately, came to me, made me rise, and, after having turned me backwards and forwards, as often as her vivacity prompted, after having handled all the parts of my dress with a most scrupulous attention,

the

she beckoned to a young man to draw near, and began
again with him the examination of my figure.

Though I shewed a diflike to the liberty which both
of them took, as the richnefs cf the woman's drefs
made me take her for a Pallas, and the magnificence
of the young man, who was all over plated with
gold, made him look like an Anqui*, I dared not
oppofe their will: but this rafh favage, emboldened
by the familiarity of the Pallas, and perhaps by my
fubmiffion, having had the impudence to put his hand
upon my neck, I pufhed it away with a furprife and
indignation that fhewed him I underftood good manners better than himfelf. Upon my crying out, Deterville came up, and after he had fpoke a few words
to the young favage, the latter, clapping one hand
upon his fhoulder, fet up fuch a laugh as quite diftorted
his figure. The Cacique difengaged himfelf, and,
blufhing, fpoke to him in fo cold a tone, that the
young man's gaiety vanifhed : he feemed to have no
more to fay, and retired without coming near us
again. O my dear Aza, what a refpect do the manners of this country make me have for thofe of the
children of the Sun! How does the temerity of the
young Anqui bring back to my mind thy tender refpect, thy fage referve, and the charms of decency
that reigned in our converfations! I perceived it the
firft moment I faw thee, dear delight of my foul,
and I fhall think of it all the days of my life. Thou
alone uniteft in thyfelf all the perfections which nature has fhed upon mankind; as my heart has collected within it all the fentiments of tendernefs and
admiration that will attach me to thee till death.

* A prince of the blood. There muft be leave from an Inca
for a Peruvian to wear gold upon his apparel, and the Inca gives
this permiffion only to the princes of the blood royal.

LETTER

LETTER XV.

*To AZA: characters of Deterville, his sister Celina,
and mother; presents made her.*

THE more I see the Cacique and his sister, my dear
Aza, the more difficulty I have to perfuade myself
they are of this nation: they alone know what virtue
is, and respect it. The simple manners, the native
goodnefs, and the modest gaiety of Celina, would make
one think she had been bred up among our virgins.
The honest sweetnefs, the serious tendernefs of her
brother, would easily perfuade me that he was born
of the blood of the Incas. They both treat me with
as much humanity as we would shew them, if like
misfortunes had brought them among us.

I do not doubt but the Cacique is a good tributary.
He never enters my apartment but he makes me a
present of some of the wonderful things with which
this country abounds*. Sometimes they are pieces of
that machine which doubles objects, inclofed in little
frames of curious matter. At other times he brings
me little stones of surprifing luftre, with which it is
the custom here to adorn almost all the parts of the
body: They hang them to their ears, put them on the
stomach, the neck, the knees, and even the shoes; all
which has a very agreeable effect.

But what I am most amufed with are certain small
utenfils of a very hard metal, and most fingular use.
Some are employed in the works which Celina teaches
me to make: others, of a cutting form, ferve to divide all forts of stuffs, of which we make as many

---

* The Caciques and Curacas were obliged to furnish the
drefs and provifion of the Inca and the Queen. They never
came into the prefence of either without offering them fome
tribute of the curiofities of the province they commanded.

bits

bits as we pleafe without trouble, and in a very ingenious diverting manner. I have an infinite number of other rarities ftill more extraordinary : which not being in ufe with us, I cannot find words in our tongue to give thee an idea of them.

I keep all thefe gifts carefully for thee, my dear Aza : befides the pleafure thy furprife will give me when thou feeft them, they undoubtedly belong to thee. If the cacique was not fubject to thy obedience, would he pay me a tribute which he knows to be due only to thy fupreme rank ? The refpect he has always fhewn me, made me think, from the firft, that my birth was known to him ; and the prefents he now honours me with convince me that he knows I am to be thy fpoufe, fince he treats me already as a Mama Oella*.

This conviction revives me, and calms a part of my inquietudes. I conceive that nothing is wanting, but the power of expreffing myfelf, for me to be informed what are the Cacique's reafons for keeping me, and to determine him to deliver me into thy power : but, till that can be, I have a great many pains to fuffer. The humour of Madame (fo they call Deterville's mother) is not near fo amiable as that of the children. Far from treating me with fo much goodnefs, fhe fhews me, on all occafions, a coldnefs and difdain that mortifies me, though I can neither remedy nor difcover the caufe of it ; and yet by an oppofition of fentiments that I underftand ftill lefs, fhe requires to have me continually with her.

This gives me infupportable torture ; for conftraint reigns wherever fhe is, and it is only by ftealth that Celina and her brother give me figns of their friendfhip.---They do not themfelves dare to fpeak freely before her ; for which reafon they fpend part of their nights in my chamber, which is the only time we

* This is the name the queens take when they afcend the throne.

enjoy

enjoy in peace the pleasure of seeing one another. Though I cannot partake of their conversation, their presence is always agreeable to me. It is not for want of care in either of them that I am not happy. Alas! my dear Aza, they are ignorant that I cannot bear to be remote from thee, and that I do not think myself to live, except when the remembrance of thee, and my tenderness, employ me entirely.

LETTER XVI.

To Aza: laments that her quipos are almost used, and begins to learn to read; sees a French tragedy.

I HAVE so few quipos left, my dear Aza, that I scarce dare use them. When I would go to knotting them, the dread of seeing an end of them stops me; as if I could multiply by sparing them. I am going to lose the pleasure of my soul, the support of my life: nothing can relieve the weight of thy absence, which must now weigh me down. I tasted a delicate pleasure in preserving the remembrance of the most secret motions of my heart to offer thee its homage. My design was to preserve the memory of the principal customs of this singular nation, to amuse thy leisure with in more happy times. Alas! I have little hopes now left of executing my project. If I find at present so much difficulty in putting my ideas into order, how shall I hereafter recal them without foreign assistance? 'Tis true they offer me one; but the execution of it is so difficult, that I think it impossible.

The Cacique has brought me one of this country savages, who comes daily to give me lessons in his tongue, and to shew me the method of giving a sort of existence to our thoughts. This is done by drawing small figures, which they call letters, with a feather upon a thin matter called paper. These

figures

figures have names, and thofe names put together reprefent the found of words. But their names and founds feem to me fo little diftinct from one another, that, if I do in time fucceed in learning them, I am fure it will not be without a great deal of pains. This poor favage takes an incredible deal of trouble to teach me, and I give myfelf more to learn: yet I make fo little progrefs, that I would renounce the enterprife, if I knew any other way to inform myfelf of thy fate and mine.

There is no other, my dear Aza; therefore my whole delight is now in this new and fingular ftudy, I would live alone: all that I fee difpleafes me, and the neceffity impofed on me of being always in Madame's apartment gives me great torment. At firft, by exciting the curiofity of others, I amufed my own: but, where the eyes only are to be ufed, they are foon to be fatisfied. All the women are alike, have ftill the fame manners, and I think they always fpeak the fame words. The appearances are more varied among the men: fome of them look as if they thought: but, in general, I fufpect this nation not to be what it appears; for affectation feems to be its ruling character. If the demonftrations of zeal and earneftnefs, with which the moft trifling duties of fociety are here graced, were natural, thefe people, my dear Aza, muft certainly have in their hearts more goodnefs and humanity than our's: and who can think this poffible?

If they had as much ferenity in the foul as upon the countenance, if the propenfity to joy, which i remark in all their actions, was fincere, would they chofe for their amufement fuch fpectacles as they have carried me to fee?

They conducted me into a place where were reprefented almoft as in thy palace, the actions of men who are no more*. But as we revive only the memory of the

---

* The Incas caufed a kind of comedies to be reprefented, the fubjects of which were taken from the brighteft actions of their predeceffors.

moft

most wise and virtuous, I believe only madmen and
villains are reprefented here. Thofe who perfonated
them raved and ftormed as if they were wild; and I
faw one of them carry his fury fo high as to kill himfelf. The fine women, whom feemingly they perfe-
cuted, wept inceffantly, and fhewed fuch tokens of
defpair, that the words they made ufe of were not neceffary to fhew the excefs of their anguifh. Could one
think, my dear Aza, that a whole people, whofe outfide is fo humane, fhould be pleafed at the reprefenta-
tion of thofe misfortunes or crimes, which either overwhelmed or degraded creatures like themfelves?

But perhaps they have occafion here for the horror
of vice to conduct them to virtue. This thought
ftarts upon me unfought; and if it were true, how
fhould I pity fuch a nation? Our's, more favoured
by nature, cherifhes goodnefs for its own charms:
we want only models of virtue to make us virtuous;
as nothing is requifite but to love thee in order to
become amiable.

LETTER XVII.

To Aza: *an opera defcribed, with reflections on fpeech
and mufic, &c.*

I KNOW not what farther to think of the genius of
this nation, my dear Aza. It runs through the ex-
tremes with fuch rapidity, that it requires more ability
than I poffefs to fit in judgment upon its character.---
They have fhewn me a fpectacle entirely oppofite to
the former. That, cruel and frightful, made reafon
revolt, and humbled humanity: this, amufing and
agreeable, imitates nature, and does honour to good-
fenfe.---It was compofed of a great many more men
and women than the former: they reprefented alfo
fome actions of human life; but whether they expreffed
pain or pleafure, joy or forrow, the whole was done
by fongs and dances. The intelligence of founds, my
dear

dear Aza, muſt be univerſal : for I found it no more
difficult to be affected with the different paſhons that
were repreſented, than if they had been expreſſed in
our language. This ſeems to me very natural. Human ſpeech is doubtleſs of man's invention, becauſe
it differs according to the difference of nations. Nature, more powerful, and more attentive to the ne-
ceſſities and pleaſures of her creatures, has given them
general means of expreſſing them, which are well
imitated by the ſongs I heard. If it be true that
ſharp ſounds expreſs better the need of help, in violent fear, or acute pain, than words underſtood in
one part of the world, and which have no ſignifica-
tion in another; it is not leſs certain that the tender
ſighs ſtrike our hearts with a more efficacious com-
paſſion than words, the odd arrangement of which
ſometimes produces a juſt contrary effect. Do not
lively and light ſounds inevitably excite in our ſoul
that gay pleaſure, which the recital of a diverting
ſtory, or a joke properly introduced, can but imperfectly raiſe. Are there expreſſions in any language
that can communicate genuine pleaſure with ſo much
ſucceſs as the natural ſports of animals ? Dancing
ſeems an humble imitation of them, and inſpires much
the ſame ſentiment. In ſhort, my dear Aza, every
thing in this laſt ſhow was conformable to nature and
humanity. Can any benefit be conferred on man,
equal to that of inſpiring him with joy ? I felt it
myſelf, and was tranſported by it in ſpite of me,
when I was interrupted by an accident that happened
to Celina. As we came out, we ſtepped a little aſide
from the crowd, and leaned on one another for fear
of falling. Deterville was ſome paces before us lead-
ing his ſiſter-in-law ; when a young ſavage, of an
amiable figure, came up to Celina, whiſpered a few
words to her very low, gave her a bit of paper, which
ſhe ſcarce had ſtrength to take, and retired.

Celina, who was ſo frightened at his approach, as
to make me partake of her trembling, turned her

head

head languifhingly towards him when he quitted us. She feemed fo weak, that, fearing fhe was attacked by fome fudden illnefs, I was going to call Deterville to her affistance: but fhe stopped me, and, by putting her finger on her mouth, required me to be filent; I chofe rather to be uneafy, than to difobey her. The fame evening, when the brother and fifter came into my chamber, Celina fhewed the Cacique the paper fhe had received. By the little I could guefs at in their converfation, I fhould have thought fhe loved the young man who gave it her, if it had been poffible for one to be frightened at the prefence of what one loves. I have made other remarks, my dear Aza, which I would have imparted to thee: but, alas! my quipos are all ufed; the laft threads are in my hands, and I am knotting the laft knots. The knots, which feemed to me a chain of communication betwixt my heart and thine, are now only the forrowful objects of my regret. Illufion quits me; frightful truth takes her place: my wandering thoughts, bewildered in the immenfe void of abfence, will hereafter be annihilated with the fame rapidity as time. Dear Aza, they feem to feparate us once again, and fnatch me afrefh from thy love. I lofe thee! I quit thee! I fhall fee thee no more! Aza, dear hope of my heart, how diftant indeed are we now to be removed from each other.

LETTER XVIII.

To Aza: fhe begins to write her obfervations.

HOW much of my time has been effaced, my dear Aza! the Sun has run half his courfe fince I laft enjoyed the artificial happinefs of believing I converfed with thee. How tedious has this double abfence appeared! What courage did I want to fupport it! I lived in futurity only, and the prefent time did not feem worthy to be computed. All my thoughts were nothing but defires, my reflections but fo many projects, and my fentiments but a feries of hopes. Scarce have I learned to form thefe figures, and yet I will try to make them the interpreters of my paffion. I feel myfelf reanimated by this amiable employment: reftored to myfelf, I begin to live again. Aza, how dear art thou! what delight do I take in telling thee fo, in painting thefe fentiments, and giving them all poffible means of exiftence! I would trace them upon the hardeft metal, upon the walls of my chamber, upon my garments, upon all that furrounds me, and exprefs them in all languages. How fatal, alas, has the knowledge of the language I now ufe been to me! How deceitful was the hope that prevailed on me to learn it! Scarce had I got acquainted with it but a new univerfe opened to my eye; objects took another form, and every light I gained difcovered to me a new misfortune. My mind, my heart, my eyes, the Sun himfelf has deceived me. He enlightens the whole world, of which thy empire, and the various kingdoms that own thy fupremacy, are a portion only. Do not think, my dear Aza, that they have impofed upon me in thefe incredible facts, which they have but too well proved. Far from being among people fubjected to thy obedience, I am not only under foreign dominion, but fo prodigiously remote from thy empire, that our nation had ftill been unknown here, if the avarice of the Spaniards had not made them furmount the moft hideous dangers to come at us. Will not love do as much as a thirft of riches has done? If thou loveft me, if thou defireft me, if thou only thinkeft yet of the unhappy Zilia, I have every thing to expect from thy tendernefs and generofity. Let them teach me the roads that lead to thee, and the perils to be furmounted, or the fatigues to be borne, fhall be fo many pleafures to my paffionate heart.

LETTER

LETTER XIX.

To AZA : *she writes more of her discoveries ; she and Celina shut up in a nunnery.*

I AM as yet so very imperfect in the art of writing, that it takes me up abundance of time to form only a few lines.   Often it happens, my dear Aza, that after having written much, I cannot myself divine what I have endeavoured to express.   This perplexity confounds my ideas, and makes me forget what I had with pain revolved in my memory.   I begin again, do no better, and yet I proceed.   The task would be more easy to me, if I had nothing to give thee but expressions of my tenderness : the vivacity of my sentiments would then surmount all difficulties.   But I would also render thee an account of all that has passed during the long interval of my silence.   I would not have thee ignorant of any of my actions ; and yet of so little importance, so little uniform have they a long time been, that it would be impossible for me to distinguish one from another.----The principal event of my life has been Deterville's departure.   As long ago as they call here six months, he has been gone to war for the interest of his sovereign.   When he set out, I did not then know his language : but, by the lively grief he discovered at parting from his sister and me, I understood that we were going to lose him for a long time.   I shed many tears ; a thousand fears filled my heart, lest the kindness of Celina should wear off.   In him I lost the most solid hope of seeing thee again.   To whom could I have had recourse, if any new misfortunes had happened to me ? Nobody understood my language.   It was not long before I felt the effects of his absence.   Madame, his mother, whose contempt I had but too justly guessed at (and who had not kept me so much in her chamber, but to

indulge

indulge the vanity fhe conceived on account of my birth, and the power fhe had over me) caufed me to be fhut up with Celina in a houfe of virgins, where we now are. The life that we lead here is fo very uniform, that it can produce but inconfiderable events.

This retreat would not difpleafe me if it had not deprived me (juft as I began to be initiated) of the inftructions I wanted, to carry on my defign of coming to thee. The virgins that live here are fo profoundly ignorant, that they cannot fatisfy my moft trifling enquiries. The worfhip which they render to the divinity of the country requires that they fhould renounce all his benefits, all intelligence of the mind, all the fentiments of the heart, and I think even reafon itfelf, if one may judge from their difcourfe. Though fhut up like our's, thefe virgins have one advantage that is not to be found in the temple of the Sun. The walls are open here in feveral places, and fecured only by crofs bars of iron, fo clofe that they cannot be got between. By thefe places, which are called Parlours, they have the liberty of converfing with perfons who are without. It is through one of thefe convenient places that I continue to have my writing leffons. I fpeak to nobody but the mafter who gives them to me; and his ignorance, in every thing but his art, is not like to refcue me out of mine. Celina feems no better informed than the reft: in the anfwers fhe gives to my queftions, I obferve a certain perplexity, which can proceed from nothing but either aukward diffimulation, or profound ignorance. Which foever it be, her converfation is always confined to the affairs of her own heart, and thofe of her family.

The young Frenchman who fpoke to her as we came out from the finging entertainment, is her lover, as I gueffed before. But Madame Deterville, who will not let them come together, forbids her feeing him; and, the more effectually to hinder her, will

not

not permit her to speak to any person whatsoever without. Not that the choice is unworthy of her, but this vain and unnatural mother, taking advantage of a barbarous custom established among the great in this country, obliges Celina to put on the virgin's habit, in order to make her eldest son the richer. From the same motive she has obliged Deterville to enter into a particular order, from which he cannot be disengaged after he has pronounced certain words called Vows. Celina, with all her power, opposes the sacrifice they would make of her: her courage is supported by her lover's letters, which I receive from my writing-master, and deliver to her. Yet her vexation so alters her character, that, far from shewing me the same kindness she did before I spoke her tongue, she spreads such a sourness over all our conversation, as renders my sorrows the more acute. Her troubles, of which I am the perpetual confidante, I hear without disgust : I bewail them without art, and comfort her with friendship : but if my tenderness, awakened by the picture of her's, drives me to seek ease to my oppressed heart by only pronouncing thy name, impatience and contempt are immediately painted in her countenance ; she disputes thy understanding, thy virtues, and even thy love. My very China (I have no other name for her, this having so pleased that it has been continued) my China, who seemed to love me, who obeyed me in all things, takes the liberty to exhort me to think no more of thee, or leaves me, if I bid her be silent. Celina then comes in, and I must hide my resentment. This tyrannical constraint heightens all my misfortunes. I have nothing left but the painful satisfaction of covering this paper with expressions of my tenderness, it being the only docile witness of the sentiments of my heart. Alas! perhaps the pains I take are useless ; perhaps thou wilt never know that I lived for thee alone. This horrible thought enfeebles my courage, yet does not interrupt my design of continuing to write to thee. I preserve my il-

lusion,

lufion, that I may preferve my life for thee. I
banifh the cruel reafon that would inform me. If
I did not hope to fee thee again, I am fure, my
dear Aza, I fhould perifh ; for life without thee is a
torment to me.

LETTER XX.

To Aza : *remarks on the French cuftoms.*

HITHERTO, my dear Aza, intent only about the
afflictions of my heart, I have faid nothing to thee
concerning thofe of my underftanding : yet thefe are
not the lefs cruel, becaufe I have omitted them. I
experience one of a kind unknown among us, and
which nothing but the equivocal genius of this nation
could invent. The government of this empire, quite
oppofite to that of thine, muft needs be defective.
Whereas the Capa Inca is obliged to provide for the
fubfiftence of his people, in Europe the fovereigns
fubfift only on the labours of their fubjects : whence
it is that moft of the crimes and misfortunes proceed here from unfatisfied neceffities. The misfortunes of the nobles in general, arife from the difficulties they are under to reconcile their apparent
magnificence with their real mifery. The common
people fupport their condition by what is called com-
merce or induftry, the leaft evil arifing from which is
infincerity. Part of the people, in order to live, are
obliged to depend on the humanity of others ; and
that is fo bounded, that fcarce have thofe wretches
fufficient to keep them alive.
　　Without gold, it is impoffible to acquire any part
of that land which nature has given in common to
all men. Without poffeffing what they call wealth,
it is impoffible to have gold ; and, by a falfe confequence, repugnant to reafon and natural light, this
fenfelefs people, thinking it a fhame to receive from
any other than the fovereign the means of life, and
　　　　　　　　　　　　　　　　　　　　the

the support of dignity, give that sovereign an opportunity of showering down his liberalities on so small a number of his subjects, in comparison with those that are miserable, that there would be as much folly in pretending to any share in them, as there would be ignominy in obtaining deliverance by death from the impossibility of living without shame. The knowledge of these weeful truths excited in my heart at first only pity for the miserable wretches, and indignation against the laws. But, alas! how many cruel reflections does the contemptuous manner, in which I hear them speak of those that are not rich, cause me to make on myself! I have neither gold, nor land, nor address, and yet I necessarily make a part of the citizens of this place. O heaven! in what class must I rank myself? Though I am a stranger to all sentiment of shame, which does not arise from a fault committed; though I perceive how foolish it is to blush for causes independent of my power and my will; I cannot help suffering from the idea which others have of me. This pain would be insupportable to me, if I did not hope that thy generosity will one day put me in a condition to recompense those, who, in spite of me, humble me by benefits with which I once thought myself honoured. Not that Celina omits any thing in her power to calm my inquietudes in this respect: but what I see, what I learn of this country, gives me a general diffidence of their words. Their virtues, my dear Aza, have no more reality than their riches. The moveables, which I thought were of gold, have only a thin superfices of that metal, their true substance being wood. In like manner what they call politeness has all the outward forms of virtue, and lightly veils over their faults: but, with a little attention, the artifice of this is discovered, as well as their false riches.

I owe part of this knowledge to a sort of writing they call books. Though I found it very difficult to comprehend what they contain, they have been of

great

great ufe to me: I extract notions from them; Celina explains to me what fhe knows, and I form fuch
ideas as I think are juft. Some of thefe books teach
me what men have done, and others what they have
thought. I cannot explain to thee, my dear Aza,
the exquifite pleafure I fhould take in reading them,
if I did but underftand them better; nor the extreme
defire I have to know fome of thofe divine men who
compofe them. As they are to the foul what the
Sun is to the earth, I fhould with them find all the
lights, all the helps I want: but I fee no hope of
ever having that fatisfaction. Though Celina reads
pretty often, fhe is not knowing enough to fatisfy
me. As if fhe had never reflected that books were
made by men, fhe is ignorant of their very names,
and feems not to have reflected that fuch men ever lived.
I will convey to thee, my dear Aza, all that I can
collect from their wonderful works: I will explain
them in our language, and fhall tafte fupreme felicity
in giving a new pleafure to him I love. Alas! fhall
I ever be able to perform my promife?

LETTER XXI.

To AZA : *her firft converfation with a religious man.*

I SHALL not for the future want matter to entertain thee, my dear Aza : they have let me fpeak to a
Cucipata, whom they call a religious man, who knows
every thing, and has promifed to leave me ignorant
of nothing. As polite as a great lord, as learned as
an Amutas, he knows as well the cuftoms of the
world as the tenets of his religion. His converfation,
more ufeful than a book, has given me a fatisfaction
which I had not tafted fince my misfortunes feparated
me from thee. He came to teach me the religion of
France, and to exhort me to embrace it: which I would
willingly have done, if I had been well affured that

he

he gave me a picture of it. According to what he
said to me of the virtues it prescribes, they are drawn
from the law of nature, and not less pure, in fact, than
our's : but I have not penetration enough to perceive
here that agreement which the manners and customs
of a nation should have with their religion : on the
contrary, I find such a want of connection betwixt
these, that my reason absolutely refuses to believe my
instructor.

With regard to the origin and principles of this religion, they did not appear to me either more incredible, or more incompatible with good sense, than the
history of Mancocapac and the lake Titicaca* : I should
therefore have been ready to embrace it, if the Cucipata had not indignantly despised the worship which
we render to the Sun. Partiality of any kind destroys
confidence. I might have applied to his arguments
what he opposed to mine : but if the laws of humanity
forbid to strike another, because it is doing him an
injury, there is more reason why one should not hurt
the soul of another by a contempt of his opinion. I
contented myself with explaining to him my sentiments, but did not attempt to contradict him. Besides, a more dear concern pressed me to change the
subject of our conversation. I interrupted him as soon
as possible, to ask how far the city of Paris was from
that of Cuzco ; and whether it was possible to get
from one to the other? The Cucipata satisfied me
kindly; and though the distance he told me there
was betwixt the two cities was enough to make me
despair ; though he made me look on the difficulty of
performing this voyage as almost insurmountable; it
was sufficient for me to know that the thing was possible, in order to confirm my courage, and give me
confidence to communicate my design to the good Father. He seemed astonished, and endeavoured to divert me from my project with such tender words, that

* See the History of the Incas.

I was

I was affected myself at hearing the dangers I was
to be exposed to: but my resolution however was un-
shaken, and I prayed the Cacipata, in the warmest
manner, to teach me the means of returning into
my country. He would not enter into particulars,
and only told me that Deterville, by his high birth
and personal merit, being in great credit, might do
what he would for me; and that having an uncle
all powerful at the court of Spain, he could, more
easily than any man, procure me news from our unhappy country.

The better to determine me to wait for his return
(which he assured me to be near at hand) he added,
that after the obligations I had to this generous friend,
I could not honourably dispose of myself without his
consent. I agreed with him, and heard with pleasure
the encomiums he made on those rare qualities, which
distinguished Deterville from those of his rank. The
weight of acknowledgement is very light, my dear
Aza, when one receives favours only from the hands
of virtue. The learned man informed me also how
chance had conducted the Spaniards to thy unfortunate empire, and that the thirst for gold was the sole
cause of their cruelty. He then explained to me in
what manner the rights of war had caused me to fall
into the hands of Deterville, by a fight in which he
was victorious, after having taken several ships from
the Spaniards, and among them that in which I was
embarked. In fine, my dear Aza, if he has confirmed
my misfortunes, he has at least drawn me out of that
cruel darkness, in which I lived with regard to all
those extraordinary events. This is no small solace
to my pains, and for the rest I wait the return of
Deterville. He is humble, noble, virtuous, and I
may depend upon his generosity. If he restores me
to thee, what a benefit! what joy! what happiness!---

To Aza : *the Priest's second visit disgusts her simplicity.*

I TRUSTED, my dear Aza, upon making me a friend of the learned Cucipata : but a second visit he has made me, has deftroyed the good opinion I formed of him in the firft : in fhort, we have already differed. If at firft he appeared to me gentle and fincere, this time I found nothing but rudenefs and falfehood in all he faid to me. My mind being eafy with regard to the object of my tendernefs, I defired to fatisfy my curiofity concerning the wonderful men who make books : I began by enquiring what rank they held in the world, what veneration was paid to them ; in fhort, what were the honours and triumphs decreed to them for fo many benefits beftowed on fociety ?

I know not what pleafantry the Cucipata found in my queftions, but he fmiled at each of them, and anfwered me only by fuch broken fentences, that it was not difficult for me to fee he deceived me. In fact, ought I to believe that perfons, who know and paint fo well the fubtle delicacies of virtue, fhould not have more, nay, fhould fometimes have lefs, of it in their hearts than other men ? Can I believe that intereft is the guide of labour more than human ; and that fo many pains are rewarded only by railleries, or at beft by a little money ? Can I perfuade myfelf that, in fo haughty a nation, men who are indifputably above others by the light of their underftanding, are reduced to the woeful neceffity of felling their thoughts, as people fell for bread the meaneft productions of the earth ? Falfehood, my dear Aza, does not lefs difpleafe me when under the tranfparent mafk of pleafantry, than when under the thick veil of feduction : that of the Father provoked me, and I did not

deign

deign to give him an answer. Not being able to satisfy myself in this respect, I turned the conversation again to the project of my voyage; but, instead of dissuading me from it with the same gentleness as before, he opposed such strong and convincing reasons against me, that I had nothing but my passion for thee to combat them with, and I made no scruple of confessing as much.

At first he assumed a gay air; and, seeming to doubt the truth of my words, answered only by jokes, which, insipid as they were, did not fail of offending me. I laboured to convince him of my truth; but, in proportion as the expressions of my heart proved its sentiments, his countenance and words grew severe. He dared to tell me that my love for thee was incompatible with virtue; that I must renounce one or the other; in short, that I could not love thee without a crime.

At these senseless words the most violent wrath took possession of my soul: I forgot the moderation I had prescribed myself: I loaded him with reproaches: I told him what I thought of the falsity of his words: I protested to him a thousand times that I would love thee always; and, without waiting for his excuses, quitted him, and ran and shut myself up in my chamber, whither I was sure he could not follow me. O my dear Aza! how whimsical is the reason of this country! Always in contradiction with itself, I cannot understand how I am to obey some of its precepts, without thwarting many others. It agrees in general that to do good is the first virtue: it approves acknowledgment, and yet preserves ingratitude. It would be laudable in me if I could reestablish thee upon the throne of thy fathers: but I am criminal in preserving for thee something more precious than the empires of the world.

They would commend me if I could recompense thy benefits by the treasures of Peru. Stripped of all, dependent for all, I possess only my love; that they

they would have me tear from thee, and become ungrateful, because I have virtue. Ah, my dear Aza!
I should deceive them, if I promised a moment to
cease loving thee. Faithful to their laws, I shall be
so to my love also; I shall live for thee alone.

LETTER XXIII.

To Aza: *Deterville returns from a long absence, and
explains to her his love in French, which she now
speaks.*

I BELIEVE, him dear Aza, that nothing but the joy
of seeing thee can surpass that which I felt upon the
return of Deterville: but, as if I was never more to
taste pleasures unmixed, it was very soon followed
by a sorrow which still endures. Celina was yesterday
morning in my chamber, when somebody came and
whispered her out, and she had not been long gone,
before I was bid to come to the parlour. I ran thither; and how was I surprised to find her brother
there with her! I did not dissemble the pleasure I
received at seeing him to whom I owe so much esteem
and friendship. As sentiments of this kind border
on virtue, I expressed them with as much truth as
I felt them.

I saw my deliverer, the only support of my hope:
I began to speak without constraint of thee, of my
love, of my designs, and my joys swelled up to transports. As I did not speak French when Deterville
went away, how many things had I to tell him! how
many questions to ask him, and how many thanks
to give him! Desirous to tell him all at once, I spoke
bad French, and yet continued to talk on. During
this time I perceived that Deterville changed his
countenance: the gloom which I remarked on his
face when I entered, disappeared; joy took its place;
and I, pleased that I could give him delight, en-
                                        deavoured

deavoured to heighten it ftill more. Alas! ought I
to have feared giving too much pleafure to a friend to
whom I owe all, and from whom I expect all? Yet
my fincerity threw him into an error which at prefent
cofts me a great many tears.

Celina went out at the fame time that I came in:
perhaps her prefence might have hindered fo cruel an
explanation. Deterville, attentive to my words, feemed
to take pleafure in hearing them, without aiming to
interrupt me. I know not what trouble feized me,
when I would have demanded of him inftructions relative to my journey, and explained to him the motive
of it; but I wanted expreffions, and fea.ched for them
in vain. He availed himfelf of a moment of filence,
and bowing one knee to the ground before the grate,
which he held with both his hands, he faid to me in
a paffionate tone; 'To what fentiments, divine Zi-
' lia, muft I afcribe the pleafure which I fee fo art-
' lefsly expreffed in your fair eyes, as well as in
' your difcourfe? Am I the happieft of men, at
' the very inftant when my fifter defcribed me as the
' greateft object of compaffion?'—' I know not,' anfwered I, ' what uneafinefs Celina can have given you;
' but I am very fure you fhall never receive any from
' me.'—' She has told me,' replied he, ' that I ought
' not to hope for your love,'

' Mine!' cried I, interrupting him, ' could fhe
' fay that you have not my love? Ah! Deterville,
' how could your fifter blacken me with fuch a crime?
' I abhor ingratitude, and fhould hate myfelf if I
' thought I could ever ceafe loving you.' While I
fpoke thefe few words, he feemed, by the eagernefs of
his looks, as if he would have read my very foul.

' You love me then, Zilia,' faid he, ' and you
' tell it me yourfelf! I would have given my life to
' have heard fo charming a confeffion: but, alas! now
' I hear it, I cannot believe. Zilia, my dear Zi-
' lia, is it true that you love me? Do you not de-
' ceive yourfelf? Your tone, my heart, every thing
' feduces

' reduces me. Perhaps I am only to be plunged
' again into the despair from which I have just
' escaped.'

' You astonish me,' replied I. ' Whence arises
' your diffidence? Since I have known you, if I
' could not make myself understood by words, ought
' not all my actions to have proved that I loved you?'
—' No,' resumed he, ' I cannot yet flatter myself of
' this : you are not yet mistress enough of French to
' destroy my just fears. I know you do not endeavour
' to deceive me : but tell me what sense you affix to
' these adorable words, *I love you*. Let my lot be
' decided ; let me die at your feet, either with grief
' or pleasure.'—' These words,' I said to him, a
' little intimidated by the vivacity with which he con-
cluded his speech, ' these words, I think, ought to
' let you know that you are dear to me ; that I in-
' terest myself in your fortune ; that friendship and
' gratitude attach me to you : these sentiments please
' my heart, and ought to satisfy your's.'

' Ah Zilia !' answered he, ' how your expressions
' grow more feeble, and your tone more cold ! Did
' Celina then tell me truth ? Is it not for Aza that
' you feel all that you say?'—' No,' said I ; ' the
' sentiments I have for Aza are quite different from
' those I have for you : they are what you call love
' in another sense. . . . What pain can this give you?'
added I, seeing him grow pale, leave the grate, and
look sorrowfully up to heaven : ' I have this tender
' love for Aza, because he has the same for me, and
' we were to be united. There is nothing in this
' that at all concerns you.'—' There should be the
' same ties,' said he, ' betwixt you and me as you
' own betwixt him and you, since I have a thousand
' times more love than he ever felt.'

' How can that be?' said I, interrupting him.
' You are not of my nation. Far from having chosen
' me for your wife, it was chance only that brought
' us together, and we could never till this day freely
                                        ' communicate

‘ communicate our ideas to each other. What rea-
‘ fon could you have to entertain for me fuch fenti-
‘ ments as you mention ?’

‘ Was any other reafon wanting,’ he replied, ‘ than
‘ your charms, and your character, to attach me to
‘ you till death? Tenderly educated, indolent, an
‘ enemy to artifice, the pains it muft have coft me to
‘ engage the hearts of women, and the dread of not
‘ finding there that franknefs I defired, gave me only
‘ a vague and tranfient relifh for the fex. I lived
‘ without paffion till the moment I faw you, when
‘ your beauty ftruck me : but its impreffion, perhaps,
‘ had been as light as that of many others, if the
‘ fweetnefs and fimplicity of your character had not
‘ made you appear to me the very object which my
‘ imagination had fo often formed. You know, Zilia,
‘ whether I have fhewn refpect to this object of my
‘ adoration. What has it coft me to refift the fe-
‘ ducing occafions which the familiarity of a long
‘ voyage offered me ? How many times muft your
‘ innocence have furrendered to my tranfports, if I
‘ had liftened to them ? But, far from offending you,
‘ I carried my difcretion even to filence : I even re-
‘ quired my fifter not to fay a word to you of my love,
‘ willing to owe nothing but to yourfelf alone. Ah,
‘ Zilia, if fo tender a refpect does not move you, I
‘ will fly : but I perceive that my death will be the
‘ price of the facrifice.’

‘ Your death !’ cried I, affected at the fincere grief
which I faw prefs him down, ‘ fatal facrifice indeed !
‘ I know not whether the apprehenfion of my own
‘ would be more frightful to me.’

‘ Well then, Zilia,’ faid he, ‘ if my life is dear to
‘ you, order me to live.’—‘ What muft I do ?’ faid I.
‘ Love me,’ anfwered he, ‘ as you love Aza.’—‘ I
‘ love him always the fame,’ replied I, ‘ and fhall
love him till death.’ I added, ‘ Whether your laws
‘ permit you to love two objects in the fame manner,
‘ I know not ; but our cuftoms and my heart forbid
it.

' it.　Be content with the fentiments I promife you;
' I can have no other. . . . Truth is dear to me, and I
' t 'l it you without difguife.'

' How you affaffinate in cold blood !' cried he. ' Ah,
' Zilia! how do I love you, fince I adore even your
' cruel franknefs. . . . Well,' continued he (after fome
moments' filence) ' my love fhall furpafs your cruelty.
' Your happinefs is dearer to me than my own. Speak
' to me unrefervedly with all this torturing fincerity ;
' what hopes have you with regard to the love you ftill
' cherifh for Aza ?'—' Alas !' faid I, ' my hopes are in
' you only.'　I then told him that I had learned that
a communication with the Indies was not a thing impoffible : that I flattered myfelf he would procure me
the means of returning thither ; or, at leaft, that he
would have the goodnefs to get my knots conveyed to
thee, which would inform thee of my condition, and
procure me an anfwer to them, that I might know thy
deftiny alfo, and conduct myfelf accordingly.

' I am going,' faid he, with an affected coldnefs,
' to take the neceffary meafures for difcovering the fate
' of your lover : you fhall be fatisfied on that head :
' but in vain do you flatter yourfelf with the hopes of
' feeing the happy Aza again, who is feparated from
' you by invincible obftacles.'

Thefe words, my dear Aza, were a mortal wound to
my heart : my tears flowed in abundance, and long
hindered me from anfwering Deterville, who kept on
his fide a melancholy filence.　' If it be fo,' faid I at
laft, ' that I fhall fee him no more, yet will I not
' live for him the lefs.　If your friendfhip be gene-
' rous enough to procure us fome correfpondence,
' that fatisfaction will fuffice to render my life lefs
' infupportable ; and I fhall die content, provided
' you promife to inform him that I loved him dying.'

' Oh ! this is too much,' cried he, rifing up brifkly.
' Yes, if it is poffible, I will be the only one un-
' happy.　You fhall know this heart which you dif-
' dain : you fhall fee of what efforts a love like mine

' is

' is capable, and I will force you at leaft to lament
' me.' As he fpoke thefe words he fprang away, and
left me in a condition which I do not yet well comprehend. I continued ftanding, my eyes fixed on the
door by which Deterville went out, plunged in a confufion of thoughts, which I ftrove in vain to reduce to
order. I fhould have continued there longer if Celina
had not come into the parlour.

She afked me, fharply, why her brother was gone
fo foon, and I did not conceal from her what had
paffed betwixt us. At firft fhe feemed to grieve for
what fhe called her brother's misfortune: then turn-
ing her forrow into rage, fhe loaded me with the
hardeft reproaches, to which I dared not anfwer a
ingle word. What could I have faid to her? My
trouble did not leave me the liberty of thinking. I
went out, and fhe did not follow me. Retiring into
my chamber, I ftayed there a whole day without
daring to appear, without fpeaking to any perfon,
and in fuch a diforder of mind that did not permit me
to write to thee. Celina's wrath, her brother's
defpair, and his laft words, to which I dared not
give a favourable fenfe, alternately tormented my
foul, and gave me the moft cruel uneafinefs. At laft
I thought, that the only way to foften my inquietudes,
was to paint them to thee, and to fearch in thy love
for thofe counfels which I have fo much need of.
This error fupported me while I was writing: but
how fhort a time did it laft? My letter is written,
and the characters are drawn for myfelf only. Thou
art ignorant of what I fuffer, thou doft not even
know whether I exift, whether I continue to love
thee. Aza! my dear Aza! thou wilt never know
thefe things.

LETTER

*To Aza: she falls sick; account of Madame Deter-
ville's death.*

I MAY juftly call that time an abfence, my dear
Aza, which is elapfed fince the laft time I wrote to
thee.---Some days after the converfation I had with
Deterville, I fell into a ficknefs which they call a
fever. If, as I believe, it was caufed by the painful
fenfations which then agitated me, I doubt not but it
has been lengthened by the forrowful reflections that
have fince employed me, and by my regret for having
loft the friendfhip of Celina.

Though fhe feemed to be concerned for my malady,
and took of me all the care that was in her power,
it was with fo cold an air, and fo little fympathy in
the afflition of my foul, that I cannot doubt but her
fentiments towards me are altered. The extreme friendfhip fhe has for her brother fets her againft me, and
fhe continually reproaches me for having rendered him
unhappy. The fhame of appearing ungrateful inti-
midates me : the affected kindneffes of Celina torture
me : fhe is conftrained by my perplexity, and the faft
and agreeable are banifhed from our converfation. In
fpite of fo much contrariety and pain from the brother and fifter, I am not unaffected with the events
which have changed their deftiny.

Madame Deterville is dead. This unnatural mother
has not belied her character ; fhe has left her whole
fortune to her eldeft fon. There are hopes that the
lawyers may hinder the effects of this injuftice. Deterville, difinterefted with regard to himfelf, takes infinite pains to redeem Celina from oppreffion. Her
misfortune feems to redouble his friendfhip for her :
befides that he comes to fee her every day, he writes
to her night and morning : his letters are full of tender

der complaints againft me, and fuch lively folicitude for my health, that though Celina affects, in reading them to me, to inform me only of the progrefs of their affairs, I can eafily difcover the motive of this pretence. I do not doubt but Deterville writes them on purpofe that they may be read to me ; and yet I am perfuaded he would not do it if he knew the heavy reproaches that always follow thefe lectures. They make their impreffion upon my heart, and forrow confumes me.

Hitherto, in the midft of ftorms, I have enjoyed the weak fatisfaction of living in peace with myfelf. Not a fpot fullied the purity of my foul, nor a remorfe troubled it. But now I cannot think, without a fort of contempt for myfelf, that I fhould make two perfons unhappy to whom I owe my life. How do I interrupt the repofe which but for me they would enjoy ! and yet, though I do them all the harm in my power, I am not, nor will I ceafe to be in this refpect criminal. My tendernefs for thee triumphs over my remorfe. Aza, how do I love thee !

LETTER XXV.

To Aza : Deterville difcovers to her that Aza is in Spain, and expoftulates for himfelf in vain.

How hurtful, my dear Aza, may prudence fometimes be! I have a long time refifted the powerful inftances which Deterville had caufed to be made to me, that I would grant him a moment's converfation. Alas! I fhunned my own happinefs. At length, lefs through complaifance than becaufe I was weary of Celina's importunity, I fuffered myfelf to be led to the parlour. At fight of the frightful change in Deterville, which makes him fcarce to be known, I ftood confounded, repented already the ftep I had taken, and waited, trembling, for the reproaches which I
H thought

thought he had a right to lay on me. How could
I divine that he was going to fill my foul with pleafure? ‘ Pardon me, Zilia,’ faid he, ‘ the violence
‘ I put on you. I fhould not have obliged you to
‘ fee me, if I had not brought you as much joy as
‘ you inflict torment on me. Is a moment’s fight of
‘ you too much to require, in recompence for the
‘ cruel facrifice I am going to make you?’ Then,
without giving me time to anfwer, ‘ Here,’ fays he,
‘ is a letter from that relation you was fpeaking of.
‘ This will inform you of Aza’s fituation, and, in fo
‘ doing, prove, better than all my oaths, how great
‘ is the excefs of my love.’ He then read the letter
through. Oh! my dear Aza, could I hear it, and
not die for joy? It informed me that thy days are
preferved, that thou art free, that thou liveft, out of
danger, at the court of Spain. What an unhoped for
happinefs! This admirable letter was writ by a man
who knows thee, who fees thee, who converfes with
thee. Perhaps thy looks were fixed a moment upon
this precious paper. I could not take mine from off
it. It was with pain I fuppreffed the joyous exclamations that were ready to efcape, and tears of love overflowed my countenance.

If I had followed the motions of my heart, a hundred times fhould I have interrupted Deterville, to
tell him all that my gratitude infpired: but I did not
forget that my felicity would augment his pain, and
fo concealed my tranfports, that only my tears were
vifible. ‘ You fee, Zilia,’ faid he, after he had done
reading, ‘ that I have kept my word: you are in-
‘ formed of Aza’s fituation: What is there more to
‘ be done? Give your orders without referve; there
‘ is nothing that you have not a right to exact of my
‘ love, provided it contributes to your felicity.’
Though I might have expected this excefs of goodnefs, it neverthelefs furprifed and affected me. I
was fome moments perplexed for an anfwer, fearing
to aggravate the grief of fo generous a man. I fought

for terms that might exprefs the truth of my heart, without offending the fenfibility of his : I could not find them, and yet was obliged to fpeak. ‘ My hap-
‘ pinefs,’ faid I, ‘ will never be without mixture,
‘ fince I cannot reconcile the duties of love with thofe
‘ of friendfhip. I would regain the friendfhip both of
‘ you and Celina ; would never leave you ; would for
‘ ever admire your virtues, and through my whole life
‘ pay the tribute of gratitude which I owe for your
‘ goodnefs. I know that, in removing to a diftance
‘ from two perfons fo dear, I fhall carry with me eter-
‘ nal regret. But . . . . . .
   ‘ How, Zilia,’ cried he, ‘ would you leave us then ?
‘ Alas ! I was not prepared for this fatal refolution,
‘ and want courage to fupport it. I had ftrength
‘ enough to fee you here in the arms of my rival : the
‘ efforts of my reafon, and the delicacy of my love,
‘ had confirmed me to bear that mortal blow which I
‘ had contrived for myfelf ; but I cannot be feparated
‘ from you, I cannot renounce the fight of you. No,
‘ you fhall not depart,’ continued he with warmth,
‘ do not think of it : you abufe my tendernefs, and
‘ tear, without pity, a heart diftracted with love.
‘ Zilia ! cruel Zilia ! fee my defpair : it is your work.
‘ Alas ! what return do you make for the moft pure
‘ love ?’—‘ It is you,’ anfwered I (frightened at his
refolution) ‘ it is you that ought to be blamed. You
‘ blaft my very foul by forcing it to be ungrateful ;
‘ you lay wafte my heart by a fruitlefs fenfibility !
‘ In the name of friendfhip, do not tarnifh a genero-
‘ fity without example, by a defpair which would
‘ caufe the bitternefs of my life, and not render you
‘ happy. Do not condemn in me the fame fentiment
‘ which you cannot furmount, and force me to com-
‘ plain of you unwillingly. Let me cherifh your
‘ name, bear it to the utmoft limits of the world, and
‘ make it revered by people who are the adorers of
‘ virtue.’ I know not how I pronounced thefe words ;
but Deterville, fixing his eyes upon me, and yet not
perceiving to look, but fhut up, as it were, in himfelf,

continued

continued a long time in profound meditation. I did not dare to interrupt him, and we kept equal fiience till he refumed his fpeech, and with a fort of tranquillity, faid to me---‘ Yes, Zilia, I know I feel my ‘ own injuftice : but can one coolly renounce the fight ‘ of fo many charms ? You will have it fo, and you ‘ fhall be obeyed. O heaven ! what a facrifice ! My ‘ forrowful days fhall roll on, and end without feeing ‘ you. At leaft if death......Let us talk no more ‘ of it,’ added he, interrupting himfelf : ‘ my weak- ‘ nefs betrayed me : give me two days to confirm ‘ myfelf, and I will wait upon you again, that we ‘ may together take the meafures neceffary for your ‘ journey. Adieu, Zilia. May the happy Aza tafte ‘ all felicity.’ At faying thefe words he went out.

I confefs to thee, my dear Aza, though Deterville is fo dear to me, though I was deeply affected with his grief, I had too much impatience to enjoy my felicity in peace not to be well pleafed with his retirement.--- How delightful is it, after fo much pain, to give one-felf up to joy ! I paffed the reft of the day in the moft tender raptures. I did not write to thee : a letter would have been too little for my heart, it would have recalled thy abfence to my mind. I faw thee, I fpoke to thee, dear Aza ! What had been wanting to my happinefs, if thou hadft joined to that precious letter fome tokens of thy tendernefs ? Why didft thou not do it ? They fpoke to thee concerning me ; thou knoweft my fituation, and I heard not a word of thy love. But can I doubt of thy heart ? mine is anfwerable for it. Thou loveft me ; thy joy is equal to mine : thou burneft with the fame fire, and the fame impatience devours thee.---Let fear be far from my foul, and joy reign there without mixture. Yet---thou haft embraced the religion of that favage people. What is that religion ? Does it require the fame facrifices of affection as that of France ? No : thou wouldft not then have fubmitted to it. However that be, my heart is under thy laws : fub-

mitted

mitted to thy underftanding, I will blindly adopt whatever may render us infeparable. How can I fear? Soon reunited to my blifs, to my being, to my all, I fhall hereafter think for thee only, and live for nothing but to love thee.

LETTER XXVI.

To AzA : *fhe declares her refolution of waiting for him in France.*

IT is here, my dear Aza, that I fhall fee thee again : my felicity increafes every day by its particular circumftances. The interview affigned me by Deterville is juft over, and whatever pleafure I promifed myfelf in furmounting the difficulties of a long journey, of preventing thee, of meeting thy footfteps, I facrifice it without regret to the happinefs of feeing thee fooner. Deterville has proved to me, with fuch ftrong evidence, that thou mayeft be here in lefs time than I can travel into Spain, that, though he generoufly left me the choice, I did not hefitate to wait for thee here; time being too precious to be wafted without neceffity. Perhaps I fhould have examined this advantage with more care, if, before I had chofen, I had not gained fuch lights with refpect to my journey as determined me in fecret what party to take, and that fecret I can truft only to thee.

I remember that, in the long rout which brought me to Paris, Deterville gave pieces of filver, and fometimes of gold, at all the places where we ftopped. I defired to know if this was required of him, or if he did it of mere generofity ? and was informed, that, in France, travellers pay not only for their food, but even for their repofe*. Alas ! I have not the leaft

* The Incas eftablifhed large houfes upon the road, where all travellers were entertained without expence.

portion of that which would be neceffary to fatisfy
the cravings of this greedy people : all muft come
from Deterville.   Thou knoweft what I owe him, and
how fhameful would it be to contraçt frefh obligations! I fhould accept his favour with a repugnance,
which nothing but abfolute neceffity could vanquifh.
Can I voluntarily make myfelf a greater debtor to
him who has already done and fuffered fo much for me ?
I could not refolve on it, my dear Aza ; and this reafon alone would have determined me to remain here.
The pleafure of feeing thee fooner only confirmed my
former refolution.   Deterville has written in my prefence to the Spanifh minifter : he preffes him to let thee
come, and points out to him the means of getting thee
conducted hither, with a generofity that warms at
once my gratitude and admiration.

How pleafant were the moments that paffed while
Deterville was writing ! how delightful to plan out
the difpofitions for thy journey, to fettle the preparations for my happinefs, of which I can no longer
doubt! If at firft it coft me dear to renounce the defign of preventing thy journey, I confefs, my dear
Aza, I have found in fo doing the fource of a thoufand pleafures, which I had not before perceived.
Many circumftances, which at firft appeared not confiderable enough either to haften or retard my journey, become to me interefting and agreeable.   I followed blindly the bias of my heart ; and forgot that
I was coming in fearch of thee among thofe cruel
Spaniards, the very idea of whom ftrikes me with
horror.   The certainty of not feeing them any more
gives me infinite fatisfaction.   Though the voice of
love at firft fuppreffed that of friendfhip, I now tafte
with ut remorfe the fweetnefs of uniting them.   Deterville has affured me, that it will be impoffible for
us ever to vifit the city of the Sun : and, after our
own country, can there be a more agreeable place of
refidence than this of France ?   It will pleafe thee,

my

my dear Aza, though sincerity is banished from it. Here are so many agreeable things, that they make one forget the dangers of the society.

After what I have said to thee of gold, it is unnecessary to caution thee to take some of it with thee : thou wilt have no other merit. A small part of thy treasures would amaze and confound the pride of the magnificent indigents of this kingdom ; thy virtues and thy sentiments will be cherished by me only. Deterville has promised to transmit to thee my knots, and my letters, and assured me that thou wilt find interpreters to explain the latter. They are come to demand my packet, and I must have done. Farewel, dear hope of my life : I will continue to write to thee, and, if I cannot send my letters, will keep them for thee. How should I support the length of thy journey, if I were to deprive myself of the only means I have of conversing with my joy, my transports, my felicity ?

LETTER XXVII.

To Aza : Celina's tenderness ; Deterville sends her all the spoils of the temple of the Sun.

SINCE I know my letters to be upon the road, my dear Aza, I enjoy a tranquillity to which I was before a stranger. I think for ever of the pleasure thou wilt have in receiving them ; I see and receive their transports : my soul admits only agreeable ideas, and, to complete my joy, peace is again established in our little society.

The judges have restored to Celina the effects of which her mother had deprived her : she sees her lover every day, and her marriage is retarded only by the necessary preparations that are making for it. Thus happy to her wishes, she thinks no more of quarrelling with me ; and I have as much obliga-

tion

tion to her, as if the kindnesses she begins again to shew me were owing to her friendship. Whatever the motive be, we are always in debt to those who help us to the enjoyment of agreeable sentiments. This morning she made me fully sensible of it by an act of complaisance, which at once transported me from tiresome anxiety to the most calm tranquillity. They had brought her a prodigious quantity of stuffs, garments, and toys of all kinds. She ran and fetched me into the chamber, and, after having consulted me upon the different beauties of so many ornaments, she put together a heap of those which had most attracted my attention, and hastily commanded our Chinas to carry them into my apartment, though I opposed it with all my power. My refusal at first diverted her only; but perceiving that the more I declined the present, the more she persisted in making it, I could no longer dissemble my resentment. ‘ Why,’ said I to her (with my eyes full of tears) ‘ why will you ‘ humble me more than I am ? I owe to you my ‘ life, and all that I have : but so much bounty is ‘ not necessary to keep my misfortunes in remem- ‘ brance. I know that, according to your laws, ‘ when benefits are of no advantage to those who ‘ receive them, the shame is effaced. It is not with- ‘ out repugnance,’ added I in a more moderate tone, ‘ that I conform to sentiments which have so ‘ little of nature in them. Our customs are more ‘ humane : he that receives is honoured as much as ‘ he that gives. You have taught me to think ‘ otherwise ; and is not this, therefore, to offer me ‘ an outrage ?’

This amiable friend, melted by my tears more than irritated by my reproaches, answered, in a most kind and gentle tone : ‘ Both my brother and I, my dear ‘ Zilia, would be far from offending your delicacy. ‘ It would ill become us, as you shall know pre- ‘ sently, to affect magnificence in our behaviour to ‘ you. I only desired that you would partake with

‘ me

' me the prefents of a generous brother ; and I knew
' this was the moft certain method of fhewing him
' my gratitude. Cuftom, in my fituation, authorifes
' me to offer you thefe things : but, fince you are
' offended, I will fay no more to you upon the fub-
' ject.'—' You promife me then ?' faid I. ' Yes,'
anfwered fhe with a fmile ; ' but give me leave to write
' a word or two to Deterville.'

I let her do as fhe defired, and freedom was reftored
betwixt us. We began to examine her drefs more
particularly, till fhe was called into the parlour. She
would have had me go with her, but, my dear
Aza, can I have any amufement comparable to that
of writing to thee ? Far from feeking any other, I
am apprehenfive beforehand of the diverfions in-
tended for me. Celina is going to be married, and
fhe talks of taking me with her : fhe would have me
quit this religious houfe, and live in her's. But,
if I may be believed . . . .
. . . . Aza, my dear
Aza, by what an agreeable furprife was my letter
interrupted ! I believed I had for ever loft this precious monoment of our ancient fplendour; I had
even left off thinking of it : but now I am furrounded with the magnificence of Peru ; I fee it,
I feel it, and fcarce can I believe my eyes or my
hands.

Whilft I was writing to thee, Celina came into
my chamber, followed by four men crouching under
the weight of heavy chefts, which they had on their
backs : they fet them down and retired, and I imagined they had brought fome new prefents from Deterville. I already murmured to myfelf, when Celina,
giving me fome fome keys, faid, ' Open Zilia, open,
' without being angry, it comes from Aza.'

Truth, which I fix infeparably to the idea of thee,
did not leave me in the leaft doubt. I opened haftily,
and my furprife confirmed my error, when I faw that
all which I beheld were the ornaments of the temple
of

of the Sun. A confufion of thoughts, mixed up of
forrow and joy, of pleafure and regret, filled all my
heart. I threw myfelf proftrate before facred remains of our worfhip and our altars, covered them
with refpectful kiffes, watered them with my tears,
and could not be difengaged from them: I even forgot that Celina was prefent, till fhe roufed me from
my trance by giving me a letter, which fhe defired
me to read.

Still given up to my error, I thought it came from
thee, and my tranfports redoubled: but, though I
made it out with pain, I foon perceived that it was
Deterville's writing. It will be eafier for me to
copy it, my dear Aza, than to explain to thee the
fenfe of it.

DETERVILLE'S LETTER,

'THESE treafures are your's, fair Zilia, fince I
' found them in the fhip that carried you. Some dif-
' putes had arofe among the crew, hindered me from
' difpofing of them freely till now. I would have pre-
' fented them to you myfelf, but the uneafinefs you
' difcovered to my fifter this morning would not per-
' mit me to follow my inclination. I could not too
' foon diffipate your fears, and I will all my life long
' prefer your fatisfaction to mine.'

I confefs, with a blufh, my dear Aza, that I was
at that inftant lefs fenfible of Deterville's generofity,
than of my own pleafure that I was able to give him
proofs of mine. Immediately I fet apart a vafe,
which chance rather than avarice, had caufed to fall
into the hands of the Spaniards. It was the fame
(my heart knew it) which thy lips touched on that
day when it was thy pleafure to tafte fome Aca* prepared by my hand. Richer in this treafure than in
all the reft that was reftored to me, I called the men

* A drink of the Indians.

who

who brought the cheſts, and would have had them
take the whole back again as a preſent to Deterville,
but Celina oppoſed my deſign.

' How unjuſt you are, Zilia!' ſaid ſhe. ' What,
' would you, who are offended at the offer of a trifle,
' deſire my brother to accept of immenſe riches ? Ob-
' ſerve equity in your own actions, if you would in-
' ſpire others with it.' Theſe words ſtruck me, and
I perceived there was more of pride and vengeance
than of generoſity in my action. How near do the
vices and virtues approach each other ! I confeſſed my
fault, and aſked Celina's pardon : but what afflicted
me the moſt was, the conſtraint ſhe laid me under,
not to endeavour to repair what I had done. ' Do
' not puniſh me,' ſaid I, with a timid air, ' as much
' as I deſerve : diſdain not to accept of a few ſpeci-
' mens of the workmanſhip of our unfortunate coun-
' try : you have no need of them, and my requeſt
' ought not to give you offence.'

While I ſpoke, I obſerved that Celina looked attentively at ſome golden ſhrubs, with birds and in-
ſects, on them of excellent workmanſhip : I inſtantly
made her a preſent of them, together with a ſmall
ſilver baſket, which I filled with flowers and ſhells
moſt curiouſly imitated. She accepted it with a goodneſs that tranſported me. I afterwards choſe out ſeveral idols of the nations* conquered by thy anceſtors,
and a ſmall ſtatue† repreſenting a virgin of the Sun :
to theſe I added a tiger, a ligon, and other coura-
geous animals, and beſought her to ſend them to
Deterville. ' Write to him then,' ſaid ſhe with a

---

* The Incas cauſed the idols of the people they ſubdued to
be depoſited in the temple of the Sun, after they had con-
formed to the worſhip of that luminary. They had idols alſo
themſelves, the Inca Huayna having conſulted that of Rimace.
See the Hiſtory of the Incas.

† The Incas adorned their houſes with ſtatues of gold of all
magnitudes, even to gigantic ſizes.

ſmile :

ımile : ' without a letter from you, the prefent will
' not be well received.'

I was too weil fatisfied to refufe any thing; and
wrote all that that my gratitude dictated : and when
Celina was gone out, I diftributed fmall prefents to
her China and mine, and put others afide for my
writing-mafter. Then it was that I enjoyed the delicious pleafure of being able to give. I did not do
this without choice, my dear Aza: All that came
from thee, whatever thou wilt particularly remember,
has not gone out of my hands.

The golden chair*, which was kept in the temple
for the vifiting days of the Capa-Inca, thy auguft
father, placed in a corner of my apartment, in form
of a throne, reprefents to me thy grandeur, and the
majefty of thy rank. The great figure of the Sun,
which I myfelf faw torn from the temple by the perfidious Spaniards, fufpended over it, excites my veneration. I fall down before it, and adore it in mind,
while my heart belongs all to thee.

The two palm-trees, which thou gaveft to the Sun
as an offering, and a pledge of the faith thou hadft
fworn to me, placed on the two fides of the throne,
continually revive in my mind thy tender and affectionate oaths.---Flowers†, birds, difpofed with fymmetry in all the corners of my apartment, form in mi-
niature the image of thofe magnificent gardens, where
I have fo often entertained myfelf with thy idea. My
fatisfied eyes can fix on no part without calling to
mind thy love, my joy, my blifs ; in a word, all that
will ever conftitute the life of my life.

* The Incas never fat but upon feats of maffy gold.

† The gardens of the temple, and thofe of the royal palaces,
were filled with various kinds of imitations in gold and filver.
The Peruvians made images even of the plant mays, with
which they would fill whole fields.

LETTER

LETTER XXVIII.

To Aza : she is in the country, at Celina's wedding.

IT was in vain, my dear Aza, that I endeavoured by
prayers, complaints, and remonstrances, to avoid quitting my retreat : I have been obliged to give way to
Celina's importunities, and we have been now three
days in the country, where her marriage was cele-
brated at our first arrival. What pain, what regret,
what grief did I not feel at abandoning the dear and
precious ornaments of my solitude ! Alas ! scarce had
I had time to enjoy them, and I fee nothing here to
make amends for what I have loft ! the joys and pleafures with which every one here feems intoxicated,
are fo far from diverting and amufing me, that they
make me remember, with greater regret, the peaceable
days I fpent in writing to, or at least in thinking of,
thee.

The diverfions of this county appear to me as affected and unnatural as their manners : they confift of
a violent gaiety, expreffed by loud laughter, in which
the foul feems to take no part ; of infipid games, in
which money makes all the pleafure : or elfe in converfations fo frivolous, in which the fame things are
continually repeated, that they refemble rather the
chattering of birds than the difcourfe of thinking beings. The young men, who are here in great number, were at firft very bufy in following and feeming
to oblige me : but whether the coldnefs of my converfation has difgufted them, or that my little relifh
for their entertainments has made them weary of
taking pains to recommend their fervices, two days
only were fufficient to make them forget me, and deliver me from their importunate no ice.

The propenfity of the French is fo natural to ex-
tremes, that Deterville, though exempt from a great

I   p 4

part of the faults of his nation, does yet participate of this. Not content with keeping the promise he has made, of not speaking his sentiments any more to me, he with remarkable caution avoids staying where I am present: so that though we are obliged to see one another continually, I have not yet found an opportunity of talking with him.

By the sorrow that oppresses him amidst the public joy, I can easily perceive that in this shyness he commits a violence on himself. Perhaps I ought to be obliged to him for it, but I have so many questions to ask him about thy departure from Spain, thy arrival here, and other such interesting subjects, that I cannot pardon, while I am forced to approve, his conduct. I desire violently to oblige him to speak to me; but the dread of reviving his complaints and regrets prevents my doing it.

Celina, entirely taken up with her new spouse, affords me no relief, and the rest of the company are not agreeable to me. Thus, alone in the midst of a tumultuous assembly, I have no amusement but my thoughts, which are all addressed to thee. My dear Aza! thou shalt ever be the sole confident of my heart, my pleasures, my felicity.

END OF VOL. I.

LETTERS

OF A

PERUVIAN PRINCESS.

—⋙⋘—

VOL. II.

—⋙⋘—

LETTER XXIX.

To Aza : she has another interview with Deterville, and suspects Aza's infidelity.

I WAS much to blame, my dear Aza, in defiring fo
earneftly a converfation with Deterville. He hath
faid but too much to me : though I difallow the trouble that he has excited in my foul, it is not yet effaced. I knew not what fort of impatience was added
yefterday to my ufual melancholy : the world, and
the noife of it, became to me more troublefome than
ordinary. Every he tender fatisfaction of Celina
and her hufband, every thing that I faw infpired me
with an indi ....ion bordering on contempt. Afhamed
to find fuch un, .e fent..ents in my heart, I endeavoured to hide the perplexity they caufed me in the
moft retired part of the garden. Scarcely had I fat
me down at the foot of a tree, before the tears invo-
luntarily fl down my cheeks. With my face hid
betwixt my hands, I was buried in fo profound a reverie, that Deterville was on his knees by the fide of
me, before I perceived him.

‘ Be not offended, Zilia,’ faid he : ‘ it is chance
‘ that has brought me to your feet : I was not looking
‘ after you. Weary of the tumult, I was coming to
‘ enjoy my forrow in peace. I perceived you, and
‘ ftruggled with myfelf to keep-at a diftance from
‘ you ; but I am too unhappy to continue fo without

I 2   ‘ feeking

' looking relief. In pity to myfelf I drew near ; I
' faw your tears flow, and was no longer mafter of
' my powers. But, if you command me to fly from
' you, I will obey. Can you do it, Zilia ? Am I
' odious to you ?'---' No,' replied I ; ' on the con-
' trary, fit down, I am glad to have an opportunity
' of fpeaking to you fince the laft benefits you con-
' ferred on me.'—' Let us not talk of them,' interrupted he brifkly. ' But hear me,' replied I : ' to
' be entirely generous, you muft liften to acknow-
' ledgment. I have not fpoken to you fince you re-
' ftored to me the precious ornaments of the temple
' in which I was educated. Perhaps in my letter I
' badly expreffed the fentiments that fuch an excefs
' of goodnefs infpired me with : but I meant . . . . . '
' Alas!' interrupted he again, ' what comfort does
' acknowledgment bring to a heart that is wretched ?
' Thanks are the companions of indifference, and too
' often allied with hatred.'—' What is that you fay ?'
cried I. ' Why do you thus wrong me in your
' thoughts ? Ah ! Deterville, what a right fhould I
' have to reproach you, if you were not fo much
' to be pitied ! Far from hating you, ever fince the
' firft moment I faw you, I have depended on you
' with lefs repugnance than on the Spaniards. Your
' gentlenefs and kindnefs have made me all along de-
' fire to gain your friendfhip, in proportion as I faw
' farther into your character. I am confirmed in the
' opinion that you deferve all mine ; and, without
' fpeaking of the extreme obligations I have to you
' (fince my acknowledgment difpleafes) how could I
' help entertaining the fentiments which are fo juftly
' your due ? Your virtues alone I found worthy of
' the fimplicity of our's : a fon of the Sun would be
' honoured by your fentiments : your reafon is like
' that of nature : How many motives then had I to
' efteem you ? Even the noblenefs of your figure, and
' every thing about you, pleafes me : for friendfhip
' has eyes as well as love. Heretofore, after a fhort
                                        ' abfence,

' abfence, you never came to me again, but I felt a
' fort of ferenity expand in my heart. Why have
' you changed thofe innocent pleafures into pains and
' anxieties!

' Your reafon now appears but in ftarts only, and I
' am continually afraid of thofe fallies. The fenti-
' ments you entertain me with lay a reftraint on the
' expreffion of mine, and deprive me of the pleafure
' of defcribing to you, without difguife, the charms
' I could tafte in your friendfhip, if you did not
' yourfelf difturb the fweetnefs of it. You even take
' from me the delicate pleafure of looking on my be-
' nefactor : your eyes perplex mine, and I no more
' obferve in them that agreeable tranquillity, which
' has fometimes paffed to my very foul. Your con-
' ftant and ill tied melancholy reproaches me eternally
' with being the chief caufe of it. Ah, Deterville!
' how unjuft are you, if you think you fuffer alone.'
—' My dear Zilia!' cried he, (kiffing my hand with
' ardour) ' what an addition does your kindnefs and
' franknefs of fpeech make to my regret! What a
' treafure would the poffeffion of fuch a heart as
' your's be! But with what aggravated defpair do
' you make me fenfible of the lofs of it! Mighty
' Zilia!' continued he, ' how great is your power?
' Was it not enough to convert me from the moft care-
' lefs indifference to love, from indolence to fury, but
' you muft vanquifh me too? Can I bear it?'—' Yes,'
faid I, ' this effort is worthy of your noble heart ;
' an action fo juft and generous elevates you above
' mortals.'....' But can I furvive it?' refumed he,
forrowfully. ' Do not hope, however, that I fhall
' ferve for the victim of your love : I will continue
' ftill to adore your idea, which fhall be the bitter
' nourifhment of my foul. I will love you, and
' fee you no more. Oh!.....But at leaft do not forget......'

The rifing fobs choked his fpeech, and he haftily
endeavoured to hide the tears which overflowed his

face.

face. Affected equally with his generosity and his
grief, I shed some myself, and pressed one of his
hands in mine. ' No,' said I, ' you shall not leave
' me. Let me still keep my friend, and be satisfied
' with those sentiments which I shall have for you
' all my life long. I love you almost as much as I
' love Aza, but I cannot love you in the same man-
' ner as him.'

' Cruel Zilia !' cried he, with transport, ' will you
' always accompany your goodness with such piercing
' strokes ? Must a mortal poison continually destroy
' the charm that you convey with your words ? How
' senseless am I to be bewitched by their sweetness!
' to what a shameful humility do I degrade myself!
' But it is done, I recover myself !' added he, in a
firm tone. ' Farewel ! You shall soon see Aza ;
' may he not make you feel torments like those
' which prey on me ; may he be such as your desire
' makes him, and worthy of your heart !'

You cannot conceive, my dear Aza, what an alarm
the air he pronounced these words in, gave to my
soul. I could not guard against the suspicions that
came crowding into my mind. I did not doubt but
Deterville was better informed than he cared to appear, and had concealed from me some letters that he
had received from Spain : in short (shall I dare pronounce it ?) I suspected that thou wert unfaithful. I
entreated him, in the strongest manner, to tell me the
truth : but all that I could get out of him amounted
only to loose conjectures, which had an equal tendency
to confirm and to destroy my fears.

However, reflections upon the inconstancy of men,
the dangers of absence, and the facility with which thou
hadst changed thy religion, remained deeply graven
upon my mind. Now did my love, for the first time,
become to me a painful sentiment ; now was I, for
the first time, afraid of losing thy heart. Aza, if it
were true, if thou didst not love me, would that my
death had separated us, rather than thy inconstancy !

No ;

No; it was his own defpair that fuggefted to Deterville thefe frightful ideas.----Ought not his trouble
and diftraction to convince me of it? fhould not his
felf-intereft, which makes him fpeak, be called in
queftion by me? It was fo, my dear Aza, and my refentment turned all againft him. I treated him roughly,
and he quitted me in a defperate fury.----Alas! was I
lefs defperate than he? What torments did I not fuffer, before I found again the repofe of my heart? Is
it yet well confirmed? Aza! I love thee fo tenderly,
can't thou forget me?

LETTER XXX.

To AZA: *impatience for his coming; defcription of
French vifits.*

THE journey, my dear Aza, feems to me very long.
How ardently do I defire thy arrival! Time has
diffipated my inquietudes, and I now efteem them
only as a dream, of which the light of the day has
effaced the impreffion. I accufed myfelf of a crime
in having fufpected thee, and my repentance re-
doubles my tendernefs: it has almoft rooted out my
compaffion for the pains of Deterville. I cannot pardon him for the ill opinion he feems to have of thee,
and I have lefs regret than ever in being as it were feparated from him.

We have been at Paris a fortnight, and I live with
Celina in her hufband's houfe, which is fo diftant from
that of her brother, that I am not obliged to fee him
every hour. He often comes hither to eat: but Celina and I live together in fuch a hurry, that he has
not leifure to fpeak with me in private.

Since our return, we employ part of the day in the
trefome work of dreffing ourfelves, and the reft in
what they call here paying of vifits. Thefe two occupations feem to me quite as unprofitable as they are

fatiguing,

fatiguing, if the latter did not procure me the means
of informing myself more particularly of the customs
of the country.

At my arrival in France, not underſtanding the language, I could judge of things only by their outſide.
As I had little inſtruction in the religious houſe, I
found the country turned to no better account, where
I ſaw only a particular ſociety, with which I was
too much tired to examine it. It is here, only, that,
by converſing with what they call the great world,
I ſee the whole nation.

The viſits and devoirs that we pay, conſiſt in going to as great a number of houſes as poſſible,
there to give and receive a reciprocal tribute of
praiſe upon the beauty of our faces and ſhapes, the
excellence of our taſte, and the judicious choice of
our dreſſes.

It was not long before I diſcovered the reaſon that
made us take ſo much pains to acquire this homage.
I find it is becauſe there is a neceſſity of receiving
in perſon this momentary incenſe: for no ſooner
does any one diſappear, but ſhe takes another form.
The charms that were found in her that goes out
ſerve only to make a contemptuous compariſon, in
order to eſtabliſh the perfections of her who comes
in.

Cenſure is the reigning taſte of the French, as incoherence is the character of their nation. In their
books, you find the general criticiſm of human manners, and in their converſation that of every particular perſon, provided he be abſent. What they
call the mode, has not altered the ancient uſage of
ſaying freely all the ill they can of others, and ſometimes even more than they think. People of the
beſt behaviour follow the cuſtom, and are diſtin-
guiſhed only by a certain formal apology they make
for their frankneſs and love of truth: which, once
over, they reveal the faults, the ridicules, and even
the

the vices, of others without fcruple, not fparing even
their beft friends.

As the fincerity which the French ufe to one another
is without exception, fo their reciprocal confidence is
without bounds. One need have neither eloquence
to be heard, nor probity to obtain belief. Every thing
is faid, every thing is received, with the fame levity.
Yet I would not have you think, my dear Aza,
that the French are, in general, born with bad inclinations : I fhould be more unjuft than they if I left
you in fuch an error.

Naturally fufceptible of virtuous fentiments, I never
faw one of them who was not melted at the hiftory,
which they oblige me often to give them, of the
rectitude of our hearts, the candour of our fentiments,
and the fimplicity of our manners. If they lived
amongft us, they would become virtuous : but example and cuftom are the tyrants by which they are
fwayed.

A man of good fenfe fpeaks ill of the abfent, becaufe he would not be defpifed by thofe who are
prefent : another would be honeft, humane, and
without pride, if he did not fear being ridiculous ;
and a third becomes ridiculous through fuch qualities, as would make him a model of perfection, if he
dared to exert them, and affume his juft merit,

In a word, my dear Aza, their vices are artificial
as well as their virtues, and the frivoloufnefs of
their character permits them to be but imperfectly
what they are. Like the playthings they give their
children, thefe whimfical people only fhew a faint
refemblance of the thinking beings they fhould appear. You have weight, foftnefs, colour, and, upon
the whole, a fair outfide, without any real value.
Accordingly they are efteemed by other nations only
as the pretty toys and trifles of fociety. Good fenfe
fmiles at their genteel airs, and coldly ranks them in
their proper place. Happy the nation which has nature only for its guide, truth for its mover, and virtue
for its principle !

LETTER XXXI.

To AZA : *injustice of the French to women.*

IT is not surprising, my dear Aza, that incoherence is a consequence of the airy character of the French : but I cannot be enough surprised that they, with as much or more penetration than any other nation, seem not to perceive the shocking contradictions which foreigners remark in them at the first sight.

Among the great numbers of those which strike me every day, I do not see any one that more dishonours their understanding, than their manner of thinking with regard to women. They respect them, my dear Aza, and at the same time despise them with equal excess.

The first law of their politeness, or virtue (I do not know that they have any other) regards the women. A man of the highest rank owes the utmost complaisance to a woman of the most vile condition, and would blush for shame, and think himself ridiculous in the highest degree, if he offered her any personal insult. And yet a man of the least consideration and credit may deceive and betray a woman of merit, and blacken her reputation, without fear of either blame or punishment.

If I was not assured that thou wilt soon be a judge of these things thyself, scarcely should I dare paint to thee such contrasts as the simplicity of our minds cannot without pain conceive. Docile to the notions of nature, our genius proceeds no farther : we have found that the strength and courage of one sex indicate that it ought to be the support and defence of the other, and our laws are conformable to this discovery*. Here, far from compassionating the weak-

---

* The Peruvian laws dispense the women from all hard bodily labour.

nels

nefs of women, thofe of the common people, tied down to labour, have no relief either from the laws or their hufbands.   Thofe of more elevated rank, the prey either of the feduction or malice of men, have no recompence for the perfidies impofed on them, except a fhow of merely imaginary outfide refpect, which is continually followed by the moft ftinging fatire.

I perfectly well perceived, when I firft converfed in the world here, that the habitual cenfure of the nation falls principally upon the women, and that the men do not defpife one another without fome caution or referve.   I looked for the caufe of this in their good qualities,. when an accident revealed 'it to me among their defects.

In all the houfes we have entered for two days paft, we have been told of the death of a young man killed by one of his friends, and the barbarous action is approved of, for no other reafon, but becaufe the dead had fpoken to the difadvantage of the living. This new extravagance feemed of fo ferious a cha-racter, as to deferve my exacteft enquiry.   Upon in-formation, my dear Aza, I learned that a man is obliged to expofe his life, to take away that of another, if he hears that this other has been talking againft him; or to banifh himfelf from fociety, if he refufes to take fo cruel a vengeance.   I wanted to be told no more, in order to form a clear idea of what I fought. It is certain that the men, naturally cowards, with-out fhame, and without remorfe, are afraid only of corporal punifhments.   And if the women were au-thorifed to punifh the outrages offered them, in the fame manner as the men are obliged to revenge the flighteft infult offered to one another, fuch perfons as we fee now well received in fociety, would not be fo any longer.   The flanderer muft retire into a defert, and there hide his malice and his fhame.   But cow-ards have nothing to fear, and have too well founded this abufe to fee it ever abolifhed.

Impudence

Impudence and effrontery are the first sentiments that the men are inspired with : timidity, gentleness, and patience, are the sole virtues that are cultivated in the women : How then are these to avoid being the victims of impunity ? O my dear Aza, let not the brilliant vices of a nation, otherwise charming, give us a disgust of the natural simplicity of our own manners ! Let us not forget ; thou, the obligation thou art under to be my example, my guide, and my support in the path of virtue ; I, the duty that lies on me to preserve thy esteem and thy love, by imitating my model, even by surpassing it, if possible, and meriting a respect founded on virtue, and not on a frivolous custom.

LETTER XXXII.

To Aza : she is conducted by surprise to her country-house ; what passes there.

OUR visits and fatigues, my dear Aza, could not end more agreeably. What a delicious day did I spend yesterday ! How pleasant are already the new obligations, which Deterville and his sister confer on me ! and how dear will they be when I can partake them with thee ! After two days rest, we set out yesterday morning from Paris, Celina, her brother, her husband, and I, to go, as she told me, and pay a visit to the best of her friends. The journey was not long, and we arrived early in the day at a country-house, the situation and avenues of which appeared to me admirable : but what astonished me at going in was, to find all the doors open, and not to meet a single person.

This house, too pretty to be abandoned, too small to hide the people which should inhabit it, seemed to me a kind of enchantment. I was diverted with the thought, and asked Celina if we were in the dwelling

of

of one of thole fairies, of whom fhe has made me read
the hiftories, where the miftrefs of the manfion and her
domeftics were all invifible?

'You fhall fee the miftrefs,' anfwered fhe; 'but,
'as important affairs have called her away for the
'whole day, fhe has charged me to prevail on you to
'do the honours of her houfe during her abfence.'
She added, laughing, 'Let us fee how you will get
'off.' I came readily into the joke, and put on a ferious air, to copy the compliments which I had heard
made on like occafions. They told me I acquitted
myfelf pretty well.

After amufing ourfelves for fome time in this manner, Celina faid, 'This politenefs would be fufficient
'to give us a good reception at Paris; but, madam,
'fomething more muft be done in the country. Will
'you not have the goodnefs to afk us to dinner?'—
'Upon this head,' faid I, 'I am not knowing enough
'to give you fatisfaction, and I begin to fear that your
'friend has relied too much on my care.'—'I know
'a remedy for that,' anfwered Celina: 'If you will
'only take the pains to write your name, you fhall
'fee that it is not fo difficult as you think to treat
'your friends well.'—'You give me comfort,' faid I;
'let me write immediately.'

I had no fooner pronounced thefe words, but I faw
a man come in, dreffed in black, with a ftandifh in his
hand, and paper already written upon. They placed it
before me, and I wrote my name where I was directed.
At that inftant another well-looking man appeared,
who invited us, in the ufual manner, to attend him into the dining-room. We there found a table covered
with equal propriety and magnificence: fcarcely were
we feated, when delightful mufic was heard in the next
room: nothing, in fhort, was wanting that could render a
repaft agreeable. Deterville himfelf feemed to have forgotten his melancholy, in order to make us merry: he
expreffed his paffion to me in a thoufand manners, but
always in a pleafant tone, without complaints or reproaches.

K   The

The day was ferene, and, with common confent, we agreed to walk when we rofe from table. We found the gardens much more extenfive than the houfe feemed to promife: art and fymmetry made themfelves admired, by uniting to render the charms of fimple nature more tranfporting. The end of our walk was a wood, which terminates this fine garden: there fitting all four on a delightful turf, we began already to indulge that reverie which natural beauties naturally infpire, when, through the trees, we faw coming, on one fide a company of peafants, properly dreffed, in their manner, preceded by fome inftruments of mufic, and on the other fide, a company of young laffes, dreffed in white, their heads adorned with flowers of the field, who fung in a ruftic, but melodious, manner, fongs, in which, to my furprife, I heard my own name often repeated.

My aftonifhment was much greater, when the two companies being come up to us, the moft diftinguifhed man quitted his, kneeled down on one knee, and prefented to me, in a large bafon, feveral keys, with a compliment, which my perplexity did not fuffer me to underftand: I only comprehended in it, that being the chief of the villagers in that country, he came to do me homage in quality of their fovereign, and to prefent me with the keys of the houfe, of which I was alfo the miftrefs.

As foon as he had ended his harangue, he rofe to make room for the prettieft of the young damfels: fhe prefented me with a bundle of flowers, adorned with ribbands, which fhe accompanied alfo with a fhort difcourfe in my praife, delivered with a good grace. I was too much confufed, my dear Aza, to anfwer eulogies which I fo little deferved; otherwife, every thing that paffed had an air fo refembling that of truth, that many times I could not help believing what neverthelefs I thought incredible. This thought produced a variety of others, and my mind was fo engaged, that it was impoffible for me to fpeak a word.

It

If my confusion was diverting to the company, it was not so to myself.

Deterville was the first who took pity of me: he made a sign to his sister, who, after having given some pieces of gold to the lads and lasses, and told them that those were the earnest of my kindness towards them, arose, and proposed to take a turn into the wood. I followed her with pleasure, intending to have reproached her heartily for the disorder she had put me into: but I had not time; for scarcely had we taken half a dozen steps before she stopped, and, looking on me with a smiling countenance, ' Tell me, ' Zilia,' said she, ' are you not very angry with us? ' and will you not be more so, if I assure you, that ' this land and this house do in very truth belong to ' you?'

' To me!' cried I. ' Ah Celina, whether it be an ' affront or a jest, you carry it too far.'—' Hear me,' said she, more seriously: ' if my brother has disposed ' of some part of your treasure to purchase it, and ' instead of the disagreeable formalities that would ' have been otherwise necessary, reserved to you only ' the surprise when the thing was done, ought you to ' hate us mortally for so doing? Cannot you pardon ' us for having procured you, at all events, such a ' dwelling as you have seemed to like, and for having ' secured to you an independent life? You, this morn- ' ing, signed the authentic deed that puts you in pos- ' session of both. Murmur at us now as much as you ' please,' added she, smiling again, ' if nothing of all ' this be agreeable to you.'

' Oh my amiable friend!' cried I, throwing myself at her feet, ' I have too lively a sense of your gene- ' rous cares to express my acknowledgment.' These few words were all I was able to utter, my secret wish having before been to have such an independency. Melting in rapturous transports, while I reflected on the pleasure I should have in consecrating to thee this charming abode, the multitude of my sentiments stifled

the expreſſion of them.   I embraced Celina, who
repaid my careſſes with the ſame tenderneſs ; and after
having given me time to recover myſelf, we returned
to her brother and her huſband.

Trouble ſeized me again when I came near Deterville, and cauſed a freſh perplexity in my expreſſions.

I gave him my hand, which he kiſſed without ſpeaking a word, and turned aſide to hide the tears he could
not reſtrain, which I took for ſigns of his ſatisfaction
on ſeeing me ſo contented.   I was ſo moved myſelf as
to ſhed ſome likewiſe.   Celina's huſband, leſs concerned
than we at what had paſſed, ſoon turned the converſation again into a pleaſant vein : he complimented
me on my new dignities, and prevailed on me to return to the houſe, in order, as he ſaid, to examine the
defects of it, and ſhew Deterville that his taſte was
not ſo good as he flattered himſelf.

Shall I confeſs to thee, my dear Aza, that every
thing on our way ſeemed now to put on a new form ;
that the flowers appeared more beautiful, the trees
more verdant, and the ſymmetry of the garden more
complete ?

I found more conveniency in the houſe, more rich-
neſs in the furniture, and the ſmalleſt trifle became
now a matter of concern to me.

I ran through the apartments in ſuch a rapture of
joy, that I did not examine any thing minutely : the
only place I ſtopped in was a room moderately large,
ſurrounded with caſes curiouſly wrought, and covered
with gold, in which there were a great number of
books of all colours, of all forms, and admirably neat.
I was ſo enchanted, that I thought I could not have
left them till I had read them all ; but Celina pulled
me away, putting me in mind of a golden key which
Deterville had given me.   We endeavoured to make
uſe of it ; but our endeavours would have been in
vain, if he had not ſhewn us the door it was to open ;
which was ſo artificially concealed in the wainſcot,
                                                                    that

that it had been impoffible to difcover it without
knowing the fecret.

I opened it haftily, and ftood immoveable at the
fight of the magnificence it had inclofed.

It was a clofet all brilliant with glafs and painting: the ground of the wainfcot was green, adorned
with figures extremely well defigned, and imitating
part of the fports and ceremonies of the city of the
Sun, in fuch manner as I had related them to Deterville.

Virgins were there feen reprefented in a thoufand
places, in the fame drefs that I wore when I came into France: and I was even told they were like me.

The ornaments of the temple, which I had left in
the religious houfe, fupported by gilt pyramids,
adorned all the corners of this magnificent cabinet.
The figure of the Sun, fufpended in the midft of a
ceiling painted with the moft beautiful colours of the
heavens, completed, by its luftre, the embellifhment
of this charming folitude; and commodious moveables,
fuited to the paintings, rendered the whole delicious.

In examining more nearly what I was ravifhed to
find again, I perceived that the golden chair was wanting: though I avoided fpeaking of it, Deterville guefl-
ed my thoughts, and feized that moment to exprefs
himfelf.---' You fearch in vain,' faid he, ' fair Zilia:
' the chair of the Incas, by a magical power, is
' transformed into a houfe, a garden, and an eftate:
' if I have not employed my own fcience in this me-
' tamorphofis, it was not without regret; but it was
' neceffary to fhew refpect to your delicacy. See
' here,' added he, opening a little buffet that was
dexteroufly funk into the wall, ' thefe are the remains
' of the magical operation,' At the fame time he
fhewed me a ftrong box, full of pieces of gold, all of the
French coin. ' You know,' continued he, ' that this
' is not one of the leaft neceffary things among us,
' and I thought it my duty to preferve you a fmall
' provifion of it.'

K 3   I began

I began to express my grateful thanks, and the admiration I was in of so many preventing cares, when Celina interrupted me, and pulled me into a room by the side of this marvellous closet. ' I would,' said she, ' shew you the power of my art also.' Large drawers were then opened, full of rich silks, linens, ornaments, in a word, of whatever is worn in the dress of women, all in such abundance, that I could not help laughing, and asking Celina how many years she expected me to live, to make use of so many fine things? ' As long as I and my brother live,' answered she. ' And for my part,' replied I, ' I desire you ' may both live as long as I love you; then I am sure ' you will not die before me.'

As I ended these words, we returned into the temple of the Sun, which is the name they gave to that wonderful closet: and, having at last freedom of utterance, I expressed the sentiments of my heart just as I felt them. What goodness! what a train of virtues in these proceedings of the brother and sister!

We spent the the rest of the day in the delights of confidence and friendship. I endeavoured to regale them at supper still more gaily than I had done at dinner. I gave orders freely to the servants, which I knew to be mine; jested upon my authority and opulence, and did all in my power to render their own benefits agreeable to my benefactors.

I fancied, however, that I perceived, in proportion as time wore away, that Deterville fell again into his melancholy, and even that Celina let drop some tears between whiles; but they both so readily refumed a ferene air, that I again thought myself deceived.

I endeavoured to prevail on them to stay some days, and enjoy with me the good fortune they had procured. This I could not obtain: we came back the same night, promising ourselves to return speedily to my enchanted palace.

O my dear Aza, how great will be my felicity when I can inhabit it with thee!

LETTER

LETTER XXXII.

To Aza: interrupted by his arrival.

THE forrow of Deterville and his fifter, my dear
Aza, has continued to augment fince our return from
my enchanted palace. They are both fo dear to me,
that I could not forbear being earneit with them to
difcover to me the motive of it : but, feeing them ob-
ftinately filent upon the fubjeft, I did not doubt but
fome new misfortune had retarded thy journey ; and,
in a fhort time, my uneafinefs, of which I did not diffemble the caufe, overcame the refolution of my amiable friends. Deterville confeffed that he had determined to conceal from me the day of thy arrival, in
order to furprife me ; but that my inquietude made
him relinquifh his defign : in fact, he fhewed me a
letter from the guide which he caufed to be appointed
thee, and by the calculation of the time, and the place
where it was written, he made me underftand that thou
mayeft be here to-morrow, to-day, or even this very
moment ; in fhort, that I have no more time to meafure, till the inftant arrives which will crown all my
vows.

Having gone thus far, Deterville did not hefitate
telling me all the reft of his difpofitions ; he fhewed
me the apartment which he deftined for thee ; for thou
wilt lodge here, till, united together, decency permits
us to inhabit my delicious caftle. I will not lofe
fight of thee any more ; nothing fhall feparate us : Deterville has provided every thing, and convinced me
more than ever of the excefs of his generofity. After
he had given me thefe informations, I was no longer
to feek for the caufe of that forrow which devours him.
It is thy near arrival : I pity him, I compaffionate his
grief, and with him a happinefs, independent of my
fentiments, which may be a worthy recompence of
his

his virtue. I diffemble even a part of the tranfports of my joy, that I may not irritate his pain. This is all I can do: but my own felicity engages me too much for me to keep it entirely hidden: therefore, though I believe thee very near me, though my heart leaps at the leaft noife, though I interrupt my letter almoft at every word, to run to the window, yet I continue writing to thee; finding this relief to the tranfports of my heart neceffary. Thou art near me, 'tis true: but is thy abfence lefs real than if we were ftill feparated by the feas! I do not fee thee: thou canft not hear me: why then fhould I ceafe to converfe with thee by the only means in my power? But a moment more, and I fhall fee thee: but this moment does not yet exift. Can I better employ fo much of thy abfence, as I am yet to bear, than by painting to thee the vivacity of my tendenefs? Alas! thou haft hitherto feen it breathing in fighs only! Let that time be far from me! with what tranfport will it be effaced from my memory! Aza! dear Aza! how fweet is that name to me! Very foon I fhall no longer call thee in vain: thou wilt hear me, and fly to my voice. The moft tender expreffions of my heart fhall be the reward of thy hate. . . . . . I am interrupted: it is not by thee, and yet I muft quit this converfation with thee.

LETTER XXXIV.

To the Chevalier DETERVILLE, *at Malta: fhe reproaches him for his fudden departure, and relates the coldnefs of* AZA

WERE you able, Sir, to forefee, without reluctance, the mortal chagrin you were going to join to the happinefs you had prepared for me? How could you have the cruelty to caufe your departure to be preceded by fuch agreeable circumftances, by fuch weighty motives of gratitude, unlefs it were to render me more

fenfible

fenfible of your defpair and your abfence? Though but two days ago wrapt up in the fweets of friendfhip, I now feel the moft bitter anxiety. Celina, all afflicted as fhe is, has but too well executed your orders; fhe prefented to me Aza with one hand, and your cruel letter with the other. At the completion of my vows, grief darted through my foul: while I found the object of my tender love, I did not forget that I loft that of all my other fentiments. Ah Deterville! how inhuman this once is your love. But do not hope to execute your unjuft refolution to the utmoft. The fea fhall not make a total feparation betwixt perfons fo dear to each other: my name fhall reach you: you fhall receive my letters, you fhall hear my prayers: blood and friendfhip fhall refume their rights over your heart, and you fhall reftore yourfelf to a family, to which I am refponfible for your lofs. What! in recompence of fo many benefits, fhall I poifon all your days, and thofe of your fifter? Shall I break fo tender an union? Shall I fix defpair in your hearts, while I ftill enjoy your bounties? No, think not of it. I look on myfelf with horror in a houfe which I fill with mourning: I acknowledge your cares in the good treatment I receive from Celina, at the very time when I could pardon her for hating me. But, whatever thofe cares are, I renounce them all, and remove for ever from a place which I cannot bear, unlefs you return. Deterville, how very blind you are! What error is it that hurries you away in a defign fo contrary to your views? You would render me happy, and you only make me culpable; you would dry up my tears, and you caufe them to flow: by your abfence you deftroy all the fruit of your felf denial.

Alas! you would have found but too much delight in that interview which you dreaded as fo very formidable! This Aza, the object of fo much love, is no more the fame Aza, that I have painted to you in fuch tender colours. The coldnefs of his approach, the praifes of the Spaniards, with which he a hundred times

times interrupted the soft overflowings of my soul; the offensive curiosity which snatched him from my transports to visit the rarities of Paris; all make me in dread of ills at which my heart shudders. Oh Deterville! perhaps you may not be long the most unhappy. If compassion of yourself can work nothing on you, let the duties of friendship call you back: friendship is the only asylum of unfortunate love. If the ills that I dread should overwhelm me, what will you not have to reproach yourself with? If you abandon me, where shall I find a heart sensible of my pains? Shall generosity, hitherto the most potent of your passions, give way at last to discontented love? No, I cannot believe it: such a weakness would be unworthy of you: you are incapable of delivering yourself up to it: but come and convince me, if you love your own glory, and my repose.

LETTER XXXV.

To the Chevalier DETERVILLE, *at Malta: farther account of* AZA's *infidelity, and her own passion.*

IF you were not the most noble of creatures, Sir, I should be the most abject. If you had not the most humane of souls, the most compassionate of hearts, would it have been to you that I should have chosen to confess my shame and my despair? But, alas! what remains for me to fear? why should I pause? Every thing to me is lost. It is not the loss of my liberty, of my rank, of my country, that I now deplore: they are not the inquietudes of an innocent tenderness that now draw tears from me: it is the violation of good faith; it is love despised, that rends my soul. Aza is unfaithful!---Aza unfaithful! What power have those fatal words over my soul!---My blood is frozen . . . . . a torrent of tears . . . . .

I learned from the Spaniards to know misfortunes: but the last is the most sensible of all their strokes. It

is

is they that have robbed me of Aza's heart; it is their
cruel religion that renders me odious in his eyes.
That religion approves, it ordains infidelity, perfidy,
ingratitude: but it forbids the love of one's near relations. If I were a stranger, unknown, Aza might
love me: but, being united to him by the ties of
blood, he must abandon me, he must take away my
life without shame, without regret, without remorse.
Alas! contradictory as this religion is, if nothing had
been necessary but to embrace it, in order to recover
the good it had deprived me of, I could have submitted my mind to its illusions, without corrupting my
heart by its principles. In the bitterness of my soul,
I demanded to be instructed in it. My tears were
not regarded. I cannot be admitted into a society so
pure, without abandoning the motive which deter-
mines me to desire it . . . . without renouncing my love;
that is to say, without changing my existence.

This extreme severity, I must confess, struck me
with awe at the same time that my heart revolted
against it: I cannot refuse a sort of veneration to laws
that kill me: but is it in my power to adopt them?
And if I should adopt them, what advantage would
result from it? Aza loves me not: Oh! wretch that
I am! . . . . The cruel Aza has preserved nothing of
the candour of our manners, except that respect for
truth of which he makes so cruel an usage. Seduced
by the charms of a young Spaniard, ready to be united
with her, he consented to come into France only to
disengage himself from the faith he had sworn to me,
and to leave me without any doubt of his real sentiments; only to restore to me a liberty which I detest,
or, rather, to take away my life. Yes, it is in vain
that he restores me to myself, my heart is with him,
and will be so till death. My life belongs to him:
let him take it from me: . . . but, let him love me. . . .

You knew my misfortune: why then did you only
half inform me of it? Why did you give me room for
suspicions only, which made me unjust to you? Alas!
why

why do I impute this to you as a crime ? I should not have believed you: blind and prepoffeffed, I should have fled to meet my fatal deftiny, have conveyed her victim to my rival, and have now been...O ye gods, fave me from this horrible image !...Deterville, too generous friend! am I worthy to be heard ? am I worthy of your pity? Forget my injuftice: lament a wretch whole efteem for you is ftill fuperior to her weaknefs for an ingrate.

LETTER XXXVI.

To the Chevalier DETERVILLE, *at Malta: excufes herfelf for not writing: farther complaints to him.*

BY your complaining of me, Sir, I know you are ignorant of the ftate from which I am juft drawn by the cruel cares of Celina. How could I write to you ? I thought no more. If any fentiment had remained in me, doubtlefs it would have been that of confidence in you. But environed by the fhadows of death, the blood frozen in my veins, I was a long time ignorant of my own exiftence. I forgot even my misfortunes. Why, O ye Gods! in calling me back to life, have you alfo recalled to me that fatal remembrance?

He is gone! I fhall fee him no more! He flies me! He does not love me! He has told me fo! Every thing with regard to me is at an end. He takes another wife, and honour condemns him to abandon me. It is well, cruel Aza! Since the fantaftic humour of Europe has charms for thee, why doft thou not alfo imitate the art that accompanies it ?

Happy French-women, you too are betrayed; but you long enjoy that error, which would now be my only good. I am killed by the mortal blow, while it is clofe preparing for you. Fatal fincerity of my nation! doft thou ceafe then to be a virtue? Courage!

princefs •

firmnefs! are you then crimes when occafion fo requires?

Thou haft feen me at thy feet, barbarous Aza!
thou haft feen thofe feet bathed with my tears . . . . .
and thou art fled . . . . . Horrible moment! why does
not this remembrance deprive me of life?

If my body had not funk under the weight of my
grief, Aza fhould not have triumphed over my weaknefs . . . . . he fhould not have gone alone. I would
have followed thee, ingrate, I would have feen thee,
I would have died at leaft before thy eyes.

Deterville, what fatal weaknefs has removed you to
fuch a diftance from me? You would have fuccoured
me: what the diforder of my defpair could not have
done, your reafon, capable to perfuade, would have
obtained: perhaps Aza might ftill have been here.
But, oh Gods! . . . . already arrived in Spain at the
height of his blifs! . . . . Ufelefs regrets, fruitlefs defpair, boundlefs grief everywhere me!

Seek not, Sir, to furmount the obftacles which re-
tain you at Malta, in order to return hither. What
would you do here? Fly a wretch who is no longer
fenfible of your kindnefs, who is a torment to herfelf,
and wifhes only to die.

LETTER XXXVII.

To the Chevalier DETERVILLE: *fhe grows fomewhat
pacified.*

TAKE courage again, too generous friend: I would
not write to you till my days were in fafety, and till,
better collected myfelf, I could calm your inquietudes.
I fee: fate will have it fo, and I fubmit to the laws
of deftiny. The cares of your amiable fifter reftored
health, and fome returns of reafon have fupported
it. The certainty that my misfortune is without remedy, has done the reft. I know that Aza is arrived

in Spain, and that his crime is complete: my grief is not extinct, but the cause of it is no longer worthy of my regret. If any regret now remains in my heart, it is due only for the pains I have caused you...for my error...for the wanderings of my reason.

Alas! in proportion as this reason enlightens me, I discover its impotence. What power has it in a desolate soul? The excess of grief throws us back to the weakness of childhood. As in that first age, so in this, present objects only have power over us; the sight seems to be the only sense that has an intimate communication with the soul: of this I have had woeful experience.

As I recovered from the long and senseless lethargy, into which I was plunged by the departure of Aza, the first desire that nature inspired me with, was to retire into that solitude which I owe to your providential goodness. It was not without difficulty that I obtained leave of Celina to be conducted thither. There I found helps against despair, which neither the world, nor friendship itself, could ever afford me. In your sister's house, even her conversation could never prevail over the objects which incessantly renewed in my mind the perfidy of Aza.

The door by which Celina brought him into my chamber, on the day of your departure and his arrival; the seat on which he sat; the place in which he denounced my misery, and restored me my letters; even the remembrance of his shadow on the wainscot, where I had observed the proportions of it, all gave, every day, fresh wounds to my heart.

Here I see nothing but what recals the agreeable ideas I received at the first sight of the place: I find nothing but the image of your friendship, and that of your amiable sister. If the remembrance of Aza presents itself to my mind, it is under the same aspect which I then beheld him. I think myself waiting for his arrival. I give way to this illusion as long as it is agreeable to me: if it quits me, I have re-

course

courſe to books, and read greedily at the firſt. Inſenſibly new ideas veil over the horrid truth that en-
virons me, and, at the end, give ſome relaxation to my
ſorrow. Shall I confeſs, that the ſweets of liberty
ſometimes preſent themſelves to my imagination, and
that I liſten to them? Amuſed by agreeable objects,
their propriety has charms which force me to reliſh
them. I confide in my own taſte, and rely but little
on my reaſon. I give way to my weakneſſes, and
combat thoſe of my heart only by indulging thoſe
of my mind. The maladies of the ſoul will not bear
violent remedies.

Perhaps the faſtidious decency of your nation does
not permit to one of my age that independency and
ſolitude in which I live: whenever Celina comes to ſee
me, ſhe at leaſt endeavours to perſuade me ſo; but ſhe
has not yet given me ſufficient reaſons to convince me
that I am to blame. True decency is in my heart.
It is not to the image of virtue that I pay homage,
but to virtue itſelf. Yet I will always take her for
the judge and guide of my actions. To her will I
conſecrate my life, and to friendſhip my heart. Alas!
when will it have the undivided and uninterrupted
poſſeſſion and ſway?

LETTER XXXVIII.

To the Chevalier DETERVILLE, *at Paris: declares
her reſolution to live free, and comforts and exhorts
Deterville.*

I T was almoſt at the ſame time, Sir, that I read the
news of your departure from Malta, and that of your
arrival at Paris. Whatever the pleaſure will be that
I ſhall taſte at ſeeing you again, it cannot overcome
my concern, occaſioned by the billet you wrote to me
at your arrival. How, Deterville, after having taken
upon you to diſſemble your ſentiments in all your let-

ters,

ters, after having given me room to hope that I should
no longer have a paſſion that afflicts me to combat, do
you deliver yourſelf up more than ever to its violence?
To what purpoſe do you affect a deference towards
me, which you contradict at the ſame inſtant? You
aſk leave to ſee me, you aſſure me of a blind ſubmiſſion to my will; and yet you endeavour to convince
me of ſentiments the moſt oppoſite to ſuch a ſubmiſſion. This gives me diſpleaſure, and, I aſſure you, I
ſhall never approve of ſuch conduct. But ſince a falſe
hope ſeduces you, ſince you give a wrong turn to my
confidence, and the ſtate of my ſoul, it is proper I
ſhould tell you what are my reſolutions, which are not
to be ſhaken, like your's.

You flatter yourſelf in vain that you ſhall cauſe my
heart to put on new chains. The treachery of another
does not diſengage me from my oaths. Would to heaven it could make me forget the ingrate! but, if I
could forget him, yet, true to myſelf, I would not be
perjured. The cruel Aza abandons that which once
was dear to him: his rights over me are not the leſs
ſacred: I may be healed of my paſſion, but never can
have any except for him. All the ſentimen s that
friendſhip inſpires are your's, and I ſhall be faithful
to them. You ſhall enjoy my confidence and ſincerity
in the ſame degree, and both ſhall be without bounds.
All the lively and delicate ſentiments, which love has
diſcovered in my heart, ſhall turn to the advantage of
friendſhip. I will let you ſee, with equal openneſs
of ſoul, my regret that I was not born in France, and
my invincible inclination towards Aza; how grateful
it would have been to me that I had owed to you the
advantage of thinking, and my eternal acknowledgment to him who procured me that bleſſing. We
will read in each other's ſouls: confidence, as well as
love, can give rapidity to time: there are a thouſand
ways to make friendſhip inſtructing, and baniſh from
it all ſatiety. You ſhall teach me ſome knowledge of
your arts and ſciences, and, in ſo doing, taſte the pleaſure
of

of fuperiority : I will make reprifal on you, by difcovering virtues in your heart which you did not know
to be there. You fhall adorn my mind with what may
render it amufing, and enjoy the fruit of your own
work : I will endeavour to make the native charms of
fimple friendfhip agreeable to you, and fhall find myfelf happy in fucceeding.

Celina, by dividing her love betwixt us, fhall throw
that gaiety into our converfations which they might
otherwife want. What more fhall we have to defire ?

Your fears that folitude may be hurtful to my health
are groundlefs. Believe me, Deterville, folitude is
never dangerous but through idlenefs. But I, continually employed, can ftrike out to myfelf new pleafures from every thing that inaction would elfe render
infipid.

Without fearching deep into the fecrets of nature,
is not the fimple examination of its wonders fufficient
to vary and renew inceffantly occupations that are always agreeable ? Does life itfelf fuffice to acquire a
flight, but interefting, knowledge of the univerfe, of
what furrounds me, and of my own exiftence ?

The pleafure of being ; that forgotten, unknown
pleafure to fo many mortals ; this thought fo fweet,
this happinefs fo pure, *I am---I live---I exift*, is alone
enough to convey blifs, if we remember it, if we enjoy
it, if we know the value of it.

Come, Deterville, come, and learn of me to hufband
the refources of our fouls, and the benefits of nature.
Renounce thofe tumultuous fentiments, the imperceptible deftroyers of our being. Come, and learn to
know innocent and durable pleafures : come, and enjoy them with me. You fhall find in my heart, in my
friendfhip, in my fentiments, all that is wanting to
indemnify you for the lofs of love.

LETTER

LETTER XXXIX.

DETERVILLE *to* ZILIA : *in anfwer to the thirty-eighth letter.*

OH Zilia! on what conditions am I permitted to fee you again? Have you thought well on that which you require of me? I was able, it is true, to keep filence in your prefence; but that fituation was at the fame time the joy and misfortune of my life. I could take pains for Aza's return; I paid a deference to your paffion for him, cruel as it was to me. Even when I fufpected his change, without giving myfelf up to the flattering hopes which I might from thence have conceived, I wrought fo far upon my mind as to be afflicted, becaufe it would make you unhappy. But Aza came, and had a fresh view of your charms. He found you faithful, tender, wholly occupied with his idea, and your defire to crown his flame. How triumphant was it for him to fee thofe unfortunate knots, the precious monuments of your tendernefs! What other heart but his would not have refumed his ancient chains? Or, rather, what other heart but his had been capable ever to break them?

Not being able to forefee his ingratitude, nothing remained for me but to die. I formed a defign of leaving you for ever, and flying from my country and my family: I could not, however, refufe myfelf the doleful confolation of imparting to you this refolution. Celina, fenfibly touched with my unhappy lot, took upon her to deliver to you my letter. The time fhe chofe for this, Zilia, as yourfelf have wrote me word, was the inftant in which the faithlefs Aza appeared in your fight. Doubtlefs, the tender compaffion of Celina for an unfortunate brother, made her tafte a fecret pleafure in embittering the moments which were to have been fo very fweet: fhe was not deceived; you were fenfible to my defpair, and even deigned to fignify as much to me by foothing expreffions, proper to fatisfy a heart which had no higher ambition than to engage your pity.

I was foon informed of Aza's crime, and then, I confefs it, my heart firft gave way to hope, the illufion prevailed on me fo far, that I even flattered myfelf with the glory of giving you comfort. That was the firft moment of my life wherein I prefaged to myfelf a happy futurity. To thefe fentiments, at once fo foft and fo new to me, fucceeded the moft afflicting circumftance. Your life was in danger, and my foul was torn in pieces by the fear of lofing you. I laboured ardently to furmount the obftacles which oppofed my return. At laft I overcame them; and flew towards you. My refpect impofed on me the neceffity of waiting for your orders to appear in your prefence. I petitioned for leave in fuch expreffions as are natural to a heart in the condition of mine. But, is it poffible to exprefs what I felt upon reading your anfwer? No, it is not poffible. How many different notions agitated my foul! how many fenfelefs projects! That of removing from you, Zilia, I had the courage to form; but, too feeble to put it in execution, I gave way to my deftiny by remaining near you. My refpect, my admiration, and my fervices, fhall be all that I will permit the ardour of my love to exprefs. Shall I be forbidden, divine Zilia, to hope in filence, that you will one day be touched with a paffion, which fhall always be as great in refpect as in vivacity?

flections, upon misfortunes that I could not forefee, and deftitute of experience, I can by no means enjoy the repofe which this charming folitude feems to offer me. It ferves only to bring back the remembrance of the cruel Aza, with all his charms. In vain I call reafon to my fuccour; in vain think of my infulted love, rewarded with ingratitude. I fee plainly that it is from time only I muft expect the calm I defire. Why was it not the pleafure of love that fuch tender and delicate fentiments fhould be referved for Deterville, who would have better known their value? But could I forefee events of which I had not the leaft idea? Aza the firft time prefented himfelf to my eyes with all poffible advantages: birth, merit, a charming figure, and the warmeft love, authorized by duty: what more was wanting to engage a young heart, naturally fenfible and tender? This heart was accordingly given up without referve; I breathed only for him; my beauty was pleafing, and I defired new charms, only that I might be more worthy of him, and, if poffible, render him more amorous. Our felicity was perfect, till the fatal revolution which feparated us one from the other.

Long abfence, dependence on others, and the lofs of his riches, have doubtlefs determined him to forget me, in order to enjoy the real advantages that are offered him, and which he cannot now hope to obtain by an union with me. Befides, how fhould he continue faithful to me, when he has not been fo to his religion? One error naturally draws on another.

But I perceive, with regret, that I entertain you only on the fubject of this ungrateful man. How weak am I, my dear Celina! What need have I of your counfel to fortify my reafon againft an involuntary love!---It fhall be fo.---I will make new efforts to furmount it.

Is Deterville at Paris? Has he accepted the tender friendfhip which I offered him? You two are all that remains dear to me. Come, and fweeten my folitude!

Walking,..

Walking, reading, and reflection shall divide our
time: and I begin to think I ought to study your
religion. Aza, whose knowledge is sublime, who,
as a son of the celestial luminary, ought to have more
lively and penetrating wit than I, has acknowledged
defects in our's, which I cannot see. I may deceive
myself in my opinion of its perfection. When I left
Peru, I was persuaded that was the only country favoured by the Sun; that our horizon alone was enlightened by it, and that all other people were in-
volved in darkness. I soon discovered my error in
this respect. It seems probable therefore, that the
instructions which may be given me by Deterville,
whose character is formed of rectitude, candour, moderation, and generosity, may make some farther impression upon me.

I will add this obligation to all those which I already have to him; on this condition only, that he
shall employ nothing but reason and solid proofs to
persuade me. I am willing to be instructed, but not
constrained. This serious study shall be intermixed
with innocent amusements, which you, Celina, shall
partake with us. But be sure to make Deterville
sensible, that he will crown my gratitude, if he
banishes love entirely from our conversation. Such
an union will be charming, if I hear not a word of
this enemy of my repose. Esteem and confidence
shall reign betwixt us, and what would he desire
more?

Come both of you, and breathe this amiable liberty, which is tasted in the country with persons that
are dear to us. You will support my weakness with
goodness: you will fortify my reason, and time shall
do the rest.

LETTER

LETTER XLI.

CELINA *to* ZILIA : *in answer to the preceding; ex-postulates for her brother.*

I SHOULD not have left you to yourself, my dear Zilia, if I had not imagined you more confirmed with regard to a misfortune without remedy; I should even have thought it an insult to you, to believe that the inconstant Aza still occupies your heart alone. In truth he does not deserve it. Could he be acquainted with your worth, and yet shake off his chains?

It is plain, that love still pleads warmly for him in your heart : But does that justify him? You are ingenious in searching out whatever may make him appear less culpable; that is an effect of the goodness of your heart, and the tenderness you still bear to that ungrateful man. But, my dear Zilia, do not deceive yourself : He never, in his love to you, felt any of those little tribulations, which warm and heighten that passion; jealousy, caprice, coldness, never entered into your engagements. Sure of your heart, he found nothing but tenderness, and equality of humour; a passion, perhaps too warm on your side, and in which there was at least no trial. Hence arose your misfortune; he ceased to love you, because he had been too happy. It is not easy to decide, my dear Zilia, which it was that prevailed with him; whether religion, or the beauty of the fair Spaniard. If it was the first motive only, he is excusable; but the two objects, united together, make me very much suspect him. You are to blame, my dear friend, to think so incessantly on this perfidious man. It is entertaining an idea fatal to your repose. Let us not talk any more, I beseech you, of one so worthless; let us forget, if it be possible, his very name. I will come and see you; I will do my utmost to direct you. How passionately

do

do I with myself able to contribute to the return of your tranquillity, and the affurances of your felicity!

I reproach myself much for having left you alone, abandoned to your reflections; but I thought your heart cured. I doubt not but agreeable company will fweeten your folitude, and I will bring with me two of my friends, with whom I am fure you will be fatisfied.

My brother is returned, and I have shewn him your letter. He is grieved to the heart to fee you still fo full of the perjured Aza. You owe to his delicacy, and that conduct, of which he alone is capable, the violence he puts on himfelf in keeping at a diftance from you. But entirely taken up with a paffion equally tender and refpectful, he does not find himfelf capable to fupprefs all the teftimonies of it. He is afraid of offending you, becaufe he is afraid that, in fpite of himfelf, fome expreffions may efcape him in your prefence, which you have forbid with the utmoft rigour. He laments without ceafing, that fentiments fo conftant, fo tender, fo delicate, to which he thinks he has a juft title, fhould be the recompenfe of one that is perjured.

You offer him your friendfhip, and prefs him to come and fee you: Is not this a real cruelty? What! fhall he every moment behold an enchanting object, for whom alone he fighs, who, by her beauty, her fweetnefs, and a thoufand other charms, muft enflave him more and more daily; and yet will you have the feverity to forbid him to fpeak of that paffion, which interefts him more than any thing befides?

He accepts, however, with grateful acknowledgments, the tender friendfhip which you offer him, fince more he cannot obtain. He is extremely fenfible, that his friendfhip would have a thoufand charms for a lefs amorous heart: but for himfelf, his paffion is too ftrong to be confined to that fimple fentiment. Being unable to recal his own reafon, I fee how difficult it will be for him to fatisfy your's. Is it not,

my

my dear Zilia, almoſt the want of reaſon, ſtill obſti-
nately to love a perſon, who neither can, nor ought to
make a ſuitable return for the ſame?

If you deſire to be enlightened with regard to your
religion, be not afraid that Deterville will inſtruct
you with tyranny: He will give you ſuch helps and
ſuch counſels, as ſhall be in your choice either to follow or reject. You know his integrity and moderation: I am ſure he will act under their direction,
though at the ſame time it will give him the pureſt
joy, if he can ſucceed. But, my dear Zilia, in order
to this great work, it is neceſſary to be diveſted of all
prejudice.

We promiſe ourſelves much enjoyment of your converſation, and will endeavour to make our's as agreeable as we are capable. This will be eaſy for us to
do, as our hearts are free from love, and filled only
with tranquil friendſhip. Deterville himſelf, whom
we have at laſt engaged to be of the party, has pro-
miſed me ſincerely, that he will not appear amorous,
but obſerve all the rules of diſcretion you preſcribe to
him: but he beſeeches you, in return, never to ſpeak
to him of the faithleſs and happy Aza. He has a right,
methinks, to require this complaiſance of you. I
know not whether it will be very difficult to you;
but it is neceſſary there ſhould be an uniſon betwixt
your two hearts, in order to form a perfect concert
amongſt us.

LETTER XLII.

Deterville *to* Celina: *ſtates his own caſe.*

AT my return from Malta to Paris, my dear ſiſter,
I received, with a tranſport of joy, mixed with fear,
the fair Zilia's letter, which was delivered to me by
your order. In fact, this letter confirms, at the very
beginning of it, her deſign to forget Aza: but, O
painful

painful and cruel tidings! it proclaims to me afresh her refolution never to replace him by another. She even forbids me to have the leaft idea of that nature. What a mortal blow, my dear Celina, was this! Have you a thorough fenfe of it? Whilft Zilia could depend on the fidelity of one fo beloved, I had no room either to hope or to complain: I could not be ignorant, being myfelf a melancholy proof of it, that a heart truly fmitten cannot entertain more than one love. That of Zilia belonged of right to the faithful Aza: but when this fame Aza became faithlefs and perjured, had not my hopes a right to revive! Yet in that very inftant how cruelly were they deceived! Dear fifter, how hard is my fate! What is the compofition of thefe Peruvian fouls? How! Is not Zilia fufceptible of that lively pleafure, which all women, may I not fay, which all hearts, enjoy in vengeance? Why does fhe not efface from her heart the very image of this ingrate, if it were for no other reafon than to fhew her horror of ingratitude! Happy, if amidft the diverfity of her fentiments, a fpark of love for me could enter. I am fenfible that my delicacy would fuffer by thofe means; but no matter, if fhe does but love me, I fhall owe my happinefs to fpite: but perhaps I may owe it to gratitude likewife. Shall I not be a thoufand times happy? I cannot help for a moment enjoying the idea.

It is true, that this beauty, whom I adore, offers me the moft conftant friendfhip, and expreffes it even with paffion: fhe particularizes all the charms of it with fo much grace and delicacy, that if any other than Zilia had offered me fuch a friendfhip, I fhould have been enchanted with it. But can the moft tender friendfhip on her part repay the moft paffionate love on mine? Feeble image of a paffion, how will it anfwer to the vivacity of that which I feel! How great will be my misfortune, if, while Zilia renders for the moft tender love the fimple fentiment of tranquil friendfhip, her heart, forgetting at laft the faithlefs Aza, fhould melt in favour of fome other than me! I fhudder

with

with dread and horror at the thought. Alas! such a new engagement would torment me for ever. To be always near the object, in which alone my felicity confiſts, and always far from felicity itſelf, is a ſituation, that inſtead of curing the evils I ſuffer, would ſerve only to augment them.

Pity me, my dear Celina, deplore ſincerely thy brother's condition, if thou haſt any idea of what love is without hope.

LETTER XLIII.

CELINA *to* DETERVILLE : *gives him advice, and expatiates on the caſe of* ZILIA.

I DO indeed commiſerate a diſtracted heart, which finds no relief either in itſelf or elſewhere. Such is your ſituation, my dear Deterville ; you love Zilia, the moſt amiable, the moſt virtuous virgin that ever was, and you love her almoſt without meaſure. The purity of her ſoul, the natural delicacy of her converſation, her beauty for ever new to your eyes, her candour, even her very tendernefs for Aza, contrary as it is to your hopes, all contribute to nouriſh in you a paſſion, which taſte and eſteem augment daily ; a paſſion ſo much the more lively, as it is the firſt you have ever experienced. I would endeavour to cure you of it, if it were of ſuch a nature, as you could ever repent of it ; but I am not ignorant, that being maſter of this fair Indian, by the laws of war, you have reſpected her beauty, her ſentiments, and her misfortunes : I know it was not your fault, that the only good, which could render her happy, was not reſtored to her, and that even at the expence of your wealth. I admired you as a prodigy, when I ſaw you call out of the heart of Spain the happy Aza, in order to return to him, with his other treaſures, the only jewel which you could not be happy without. This was the very height of generoſity.

In

In the mean time, by an unexampled turn of fortune, when the infidelity of Aza rendered your benefits uſeleſs, and you had more right than ever to hope, the unforeſeen conſtancy of Zilia for an ungrateful man, adds the laſt and ſevereſt ſtroke to your misfortunes.

But, my dear brother, while I indulge your grief, and lament the fatality of your ſtars, ſuffer me to inform you, that you make your caſe worſe than it really is.—The anxiety of your heart, doubtleſs, prevents your ſeeing the leaſt glimpſe of hope: but perhaps the indifference, in which you formerly lived, keeps you ignorant of the reſources which are ſtill left you by fortune. As a woman, I ſhould be tempted ſtill to leave you partly in ignorance; but as a ſiſter, I cannot take ſuch an unkind reſolution. Hear me then, my dear Deterville. Aza was naturally the only object that Zilia could be attached to. A prince, tender, young, and charming; and Zilia in all the force and ſweetneſs of her firſt fires, united by taſte and by duty, and by the virtue which ennobled both. A hideous miſhap, a cruel revolution ſeparates them, and enlivens the image of that felicity of which they ſee themſelves fatally deprived. Repreſent to yourſelf how much force even deſpair muſt add to a paſſion before ſo warm and ſo legitimate. It was a heart new in love, full of fire, given up for the firſt time, and which did not know a more ſenſible pleaſure, than that of adhering to the object it had choſen: in ſhort, it was a heart, amorous to exceſs, inflamed by difficulty, and which, at the very brink of felicity, ſaw itſelf in that inſtant ſnatched from the expected enjoyment. My dear brother, put yourſelf for a moment in the place of Zilia: is it poſſible that any other lover could make her ſo ſoon forget a bridegroom that was ſo dear to her, and reſtore her to tranquillity? Reflect on the nobleneſs of her ſoul, and you will conceive that a heart ſo generous, may be capable of carrying her attachment beyond the bounds of ordinary ſenſibility, and of continuing to love an object which it is ſure never to poſſeſs. This is ſuch a muſical ſtring, as ſounds a long time after it has been once briſkly touched.

But do you not ſee, my dear Deterville, that this ſentiment is too contrary to nature to be durable? Do you doubt whether Zilia, when ſhe comes to reflect more quietly, will perceive the injuſtice of Aza, the weight of his indifference, and the inutility of loving without return? Maintained hitherto in her tenderneſs, by a kind of ſorcery, the illuſion ſhe puts on herſelf will ſoon diſſipate, the image of Aza will in a ſhort time become burthenſome, and then her heart, void of intereſt and employment, will with difficulty ſupport itſelf in ſuch a ſtate of inaction. A tireſome ſtate of languor is an inſupportable burthen for an active ſoul. Zilia will wiſh for ſome pretence to get rid of it, and what pretence will be more happy for you both, than that of gratitude? Zilia profeſſes her acknowledgments to you, and is fully ſenſible how much ſhe owes to your generous proceedings.

I come now to the friendſhip which ſhe offers you. —By your refuſing this friendſhip, it ſhould ſeem to be offenſive, or at leaſt unpleaſant to you. You look upon it is a ſentiment too weak to anſwer to the vivacity of your love. It ſeems like a payment in counterfeit coin; and you reject it becauſe it is not abſolute and complete love: but, pray, dear brother, is it the name only that you would obtain? For my part, I cannot help thinking ſo: for the friendſhip of Zilia ought to inſpire you with leſs repugnance. Let me tell you, even this ought to charm you. Why do you oblige me here to diſcloſe the great ſecrets of the fair ſex? Know, that this ſentiment of friendſhip, ſo ſweet among men, ſo rare among women, is always the moſt lively betwixt perſons of different ſexes. Men love one another with cordiality, women love each other with diffidence; but two perſons of the two ſexes add to the taſte of friendſhip, a ſpark of that fire which nature never fails to inſpire. A ſprout of paſſion will attend the very birth of this friendſhip, ſo pure in appearance;

pearance; as such sort of friends are fully enough sensible. Let them both keep mutually upon their guard,
it matters not: all their precautions will make no
change in the imperceptible progress of nature, and
they will soon be surprised, that they are fallen in love
with each other, without perceiving it.

The friendship offered you then, my dear Deterville,
is, in my opinion, the first act of that interesting play,
of which you so much desire to see the unravelling;
it is the first discovery of the heart, and since that is
favourable to you, have you any room to complain?

It is true, that the name of friendship spreads a veil,
which hides a part from your sight: but it is a veil
wrought by the hands of love, made only to deceive
jealous eyes, but which hides nothing from eyes that
can penetrate, nor long conceals the truth from him
who is the object of it. Do you not now confess, my
dear brother, that I had room to be surprised, when I
heard you complain so bitterly of the only part that
Zilia ought to have taken? Reflect upon it well, and
you will be of my sentiment. Can there be a more
happy method, a method better adapted to the delicacy of you both?

Would you not always have the better opinion of a
lady, who chooses to be the more reserved, to make
your happiness the more complete? Who, by giving
your passion a reasonable character, intends to refine
and increase your pleasure?

Indeed, my brother, you are obliged to Zilia, who,
in the way of friendship, is preparing for you pleasures more ecstatic than you proposed for yourself: she
neither dared, nor ought, to make you a return of passion in the manner that you desired. You must con-
sult the fair sex for sentiments of this nature: and be
not ashamed that the women are here beforehand with
you; since without them, the men would perhaps be
ignorant in the finesses of the art of love. Women
are allowed, as a natural consequence of the temper of
their hearts, to have more suppleness of genius than

men.   I do not suppose any artifice to enter into this
art of love, of which I am speaking: these two characters, as much as they resemble one another, ought
to be distinguished.   All the women of wit love with
art, but not all with artifice.   As to your dear Zilia,
her heart is honest, noble, and elevated; but she is ingenuous in the most fine and subtle manner of any woman I know.   That heart of her's, which is at present
wholly taken up with the most tender and virtuous
passion, but a passion cruelly deceived, you will at last
find to be reserved for you.   Allow only a reasonable
term to Zilia for grief, and, without complaining,
leave time to destroy in her that idea of glory which
flatters her hitherto. ·

That singular honour of remaining faithful to her
first ties, even when they are broken without possibi-
lity of a re-union, is a sentiment which certainly she
has not learned among us: she will therefore at last
give way to our example.   Being then free, fearing
liberty through a habitude of not enjoying it, and
sensible at the same time of your generous cares; the
friendship, which she now regards only as a sweet
sympathy, will want but one advance further to become love: and that miracle will be accomplished
without her perceiving it.

My dear Deterville, what a charming prospect lies
here before you! I think you must see enough of it
to engage you, without the least difficulty, to accept·
the party which Zilia proposes to you with so good a
grace.   From your solicitudes, disinterested in appearance, and more still from the nature of a female
heart, expect the felicity of which you began to
despair.

LETTER XLIV.

ZILIA *to* DETERVILLE : *complains of* CELINA's *letter*

AFTER the lofs of Aza, I could never have
thought, Sir, that new troubles would have reached
my heart. But now, by fatal experience, I perceive
the contrary, from a difcovery I made accidentally,
and which plunges me again into the moft cruel perplexity. Your fifter came to fee me yefterday. After
her departure I found a paper in my chamber. I
opened it : but how great was my furprife to know
her hand, in a letter addrelfed to you, in which, after
blaming you for not accepting my offers, fhe under-
takes to perfuade you by motives very different from
mine ! Who could have thought that the ever-tender,
the ever-generous Celina, my only confolation in the
bitternefs of my foul, would have proved perfidious ?
After I have given myfelf up entirely to the fweetnefs
of her friendfhip, and had not the leaft referve in my
fincere love to her, I learn that fhe does not love me
without diftruft. If your fifter, at the beginning of
this fatal letter, loads me with praifes, doubtlefs they
do not flow fo much from her own fentiments, as from
her fear of difpleafing you : for on what does fhe pretend to found your hope, if not upon the want of folidity in thefe virtues which fhe attributes to me ? In
revealing to you the fecrets of her fex, her art, or rather artifice, does not turn to the advantage of her
heart. Miftaken notion! does fhe think the virgins
devoted to the Sun, and educated in his temple, are to
be judged of by the general diftinction fhe gives of the
character of women ? Is there but one model, one rule
to form a judgment by? The creator, who diverfifies
his works in a thoufand manners, who imparts to
every country fome particular property, who gives to
us all phyfiognomies fo various and different, has he
decreed

decreed that the characters of the mind should be every
where alike, and that all reasonable beings should think
in the same manner? For my part, I cannot easily be
persuaded of this. Besides, what reason has she to give
to the men such happy prerogatives? Does she believe
they have a more ample portion of the breath of the
divinity? We have in Peru, such an opinion of the
divine Amutas, whose sublime knowledge and habi-
tudes, consecrated to virtue, elevate them above ordinary men; but for other men, if they have passions
which are common to them, we acknowledge in them
virtues also which conduct and rectify those passions,
and we judge of them from their actions, and not from
any presupposed weaknesses.

How could she undertake to persuade you, that there
was so little firmness in my sentiments? Certainly she
has not learned this from what has passed. My heart,
formed to frankness from my infancy, never strove to
persuade the unfaithful Aza of the sincerity of my
fires, any other way than by the vivacity with which
they were expressed.

I am ignorant, and would ever be ignorant of that
art, which degrades women much more than it sets off
their charms: it only proves their weakness, their vanity, and their diffidence of the object they would
enslave. Nature knows not this art, nor ever strives
to adorn the graces, and add charms to virtue.

Vainly doth Celina pretend to distinguish art from
artifice: I am not imposed upon by that idea. Does
she seek for disguise when it is her interest to hide nothing? Could one dare to confess, without a blush, that
one had taken great pains to lead another into error?

I hope all from the generosity of your heart. Worthy as you are to have been born among us, I am sure
no injurious suspicion has yet entered your soul; and
I should be very sorry to have you see this wicked
letter, left it should induce you to suspect. But should
I, Deterville, be worthy your goodness, if the too
credulous Celina thought justly?

As

As you are too virtuous to think I aim at glory in performing my duty, do not expect that either time, or the weakness of my sex, will make any change in me. United with Aza, in ties which death only should have diffolved, no object can difengage me from him. Yet come, Sir, enjoy the tranquil fruits which gratitude offers you; come, and at once enlighten and adorn my understanding.

Difengaged from tumultous passions, you will find that friendship alone is worthy to fill our hearts, and alone able to make our destiny perfectly happy.

LETTER XLV.

DETERVILLE *to* ZILIA : *he accepts her simple friendship.*

I WAS fet out, adorable Zilia, in the firm refolution to forget you, as the only relief to my pains I could think of. A long abfence, I prefumed, might work this miracle. But, alas! the anger infpired by a tender fentiment is foon ftifled by its own principle. I am here returned, more amorous and as ill-treated as ever, in fpite of the glimmerings of hope which the infidelity of Aza had kindled in my mind. My fituation gives me more right than ever to complain : but how cruel foever your manner of thinking be to me, it ftill deprives me of liberty. You bind me to you in fo engaging a manner, by the tender friendship you offer me, that though the bounds you prefcribe to it appear to me a fpecies of ingratitude, I perceive that my complaints, fhould I now make them, would become unjuft.

While I fubmit to the rigour of your laws, my heart dares ftill to preferve the hope of mortifying that rigour. Pardon my diforder and my fincerity : I exprefs the fimple notions of my heart; I am pleafed with thefe illufions, and forry when my reafon returns to

convince

convince me of my rafhnefs : then I blufh for a moment ; but foon the ideas of a happy futurity triumph.
Such is my weaknefs ! a mortifying reflection for me,
but a reflection that raifes fo much the more the glory
of the daughter of the Sun.

In your prefence, fair Zilia, one of your looks will
recal the refpect that is due to you : my ardour to
pleafe you will raife me above fenfe, and you fhall be
the rule of my manners. Bound and united together
only by the fentiments of the foul, and fimilitude of
genius, we fhall have nothing to fear from thofe dif-
gufts, which the anxiety of the paffions drag along
with them. Our quiet and unweary days, like a perpetual fpring, when all feems to ftart frefh out of the
hands of nature, fhall flow in perfect felicity ; we fhall
enjoy mutually the benefits of this nature, and crown
with it our innocence. If we at any time fpeak of
Aza, it fhall only be to recal and complain of his ingratitude. Perhaps deftiny alone was culpable of his
change. But however that may be, he was no longer
worthy of the virgin of the Sun, after he had breathed
the native air of the cruel enemies of Peru.

Let me beg you to bear no ill-will to my fifter ; her
tendernefs for me, and her fenfe of my fituation, have
made her imagine all the reafons that you have feen, in
order to comfort me, and give a new birth to my hope :
this motive ought to be her excufe. Promife me to
pardon her, divine Zilia : there fhould be nothing to
imbitter the fweets of that charming fociety, which
we propofe to form in your company.

In this hope I fet out to come and throw myfelf at
your feet : I will look upon this new habitation as the
temple of the Sun : I will there refpectfully adore the
luminary that enlightens it, and the object of all my
cares fhall be, to render you inceffantly the moft pure
and moft fubmiffive homage.

SEQUEL

TO THE

PERUVIAN PRINCESS.

CONTAINING THE

LETTERS OF AZA.

THE reading of the Peruvian Letters made me recollect that I had seen in Spain, some years since, a Collection of Letters by a Peruvian, whose history has since appeared to me strongly to resemble that of Zilia. I procured that manuscript, and I found that they were the very letters of Aza, translated into Spanish. We are, doubtless, obliged to Kanhuiscap, the friend of Aza, to whom the principal part of these letters are addressed, for their translation from the Peruvian. I found a concern for Aza excited in me by reading these letters, that engaged me to undertake their translation. I perceived, with joy, those odious ideas effaced from my mind, which Zilia had given me, of a prince more unfortunate than inconstant. I imagine that others will experience the same pleasure: for, to see virtue justified is at all times pleasing.

'There are many who will, perhaps, think it a crime in Aza, to have described, under the name of Spanish manners, those failings, and even vices, that are peculiar to the French nation. How specious soever this charge may appear, it will be easily liquidated, if we properly confider with M. Fontenelle, that a native of England and France, are countrymen at Peking.

king. I dare not flatter myfelf with having painted, in their proper colours, thofe noble images, thofe grand and beautiful ideas, that are to be found in the Spanifh original: I might impute it to the difference of the two languages, and to the common lot of tranflations ; the reader, perhaps, will impute it to me ; and we may both of us be right in our fentiments.

LETTERS OF AZA.

LETTER I.

To ZILIA : AZA *informs* ZILIA *of the hope he enter-*
tains of soon beholding her again; and of the efforts
that he made to oppose the brutal violence of the
Spaniards.

MAY thy tears be diffipated like the dew before the
rifing fun! May thy fetters, changed into flowers, fall
at thy feet! and by the vivacity of their colours exprefs the ardency of my love, more glowing than that
divine luminary which gave it birth. Zilia, difmifs
thy fears—Aza ftill lives : that is, for ever loves thee.
  Our miferies have an end. The happy moment approaches that fhall unite us for ever. O divine felicity! Why do we pant for thy enjoyment?
  The predictions of Viracocha are ftill unaccom-
plifhed. I am now on the auguft throne of Manco-
Capa, and Zilia is not by my fide. I reign, and thou
art loaded with fetters! Be comforted, thou tender
object of my ardent affections. The Sun has too
fully proved our love ; he now prepares to crown it
with felicity. Thefe knots, the weak interpreters of
our fentiments : thefe knots, whofe ufe I blefs, but
whofe fate I envy, fhall behold thee free. From out
thy frightful prifon thou fhalt fly to my arms. As
the dove, efcaped from the talons. of the vulture, flies
to participate of happinefs with her faithful companion, fo fhalt thou repofe in my heart, yet trembling
with agitation, thy paft afflictions; thy tendernefs and

my

my felicity. What joy! what tranfport! To drown
thy miferies in blifs! Thou fhalt fee at thy feet thofe
brutal mafters of the thunder: and even thofe hands
which have loaded thee with fetters, fhall aid in feat-
ing thee on the throne.

But why fhould the remembrance of my misfortunes pollute fo pure a happinefs? Why muft I remind
thee of miferies that are no more? Do we not depre-
ciate the favours of the gods, when we negleft to enjoy them in their full extent? Not to forget our mif-
fortunes is in a manner to merit them. Yet you
defire, my dear Zilia, that I fhould add to my afflictions the difgrace of having deferved them. I love
thee—I can tell it thee---I foon again fhall behold
thee: what new éclaircifiement can I give thee of my
fate? Can I defcribe what is paft, when I am not able
to exprefs the fentiments that at this moment agitate
my foul!....But what do I fay? Zilia, you will
have it fo.

Remember then, if you can do it and yet live, that
day, that horrid day, whofe aurora was refplendent
with joy.

The Sun, in the fulnefs of his glory, fpread over my
vilage the fame rays with which he illuminated thine.
Tranfports of joy, and flames of love, enrapt my heart.
My foul was loft in that divinity from whom it de-
rives it being. My eyes fparkled with the fires they
received from thine, and fpoke a thoufand defires.
Reftrained by the decorum of ceremonies, I went to
the temple: but my heart flew thither. There I beheld thee; more fair than the morning ftar, more
blooming than the new blown rofe; accufing the Cu-
ciparas of delay; and to me tenderly lamenting the
obftacle by which we were yet feparated. When, in
a moment, O dreadful remembrance! the lightnings
flafhed, the thunder roared. At the tremendous alarm
all around me, I fell to the earth. Proftrate I adored
the fovereign Yalpor. I implored for thee. The
peals were redoubled.....they relented....;...they
ceafed.

ceafed. I rofe, trembling for thy fafety. What horror! what a dreadful profpect! furrounded by a cloud of fulphur, by flames, and by blood; in a frightful confufion, my eyes faw nothing but death; my ears heard nothing but fcreams; my heart fought nothing but thee; and every object told it thou wert loft. I ftill hear the thunder that ftruck thee: I fee thee pale, disfigured; thy bofom fmeared with blood and duft; a cruel fire devours thee.

The clouds difappear: the obfcurity is difperfed.— Can you believe it, Zilia? It was not the great Yalpor. The gods are not fo cruel. Thofe barbarians, the ufurpers of their power, had ufed it to our deftruction. No fooner did I difcover the detefted crew, than I fprang amidft them. Love, and the gods whofe powers they had profaned, lent me their aid. Thy prefence augmented it. I bore down all before me. Yet a moment, and I had fecured thee: but they bore you through the facred portal, and you vanifhed from my fight. Grief feized my foul: defpair drew tears from my eyes. Diftracted with rage, I darted on them. They furrounded me. By the fury of the affault, my very arms were deftroyed. Exhaufted by the violence of my efforts, and overpowered by numbers, I fell upon the profaned bodies of my anceftors*. There my blood and my tears were ignominioufly fhed amidft thy expiring companions; even on thofe garlands which thy hands had woven, and with which thou fhouldft have crowned my head. A mortal coldnefs feized my fenfes. My fight grew dim, it vanifhed. I ceafed to live, but could not ceafe to love thee.

Doubtlefs it was love, and the hopes of avenging thy injuries, my dear Zilia, that reftored me to life. I found myfelf in my palace, furrounded by my attendants. Fury was fucceeded by defpondency: I

* The Peruvians placed the embalmed bodies of their kings in their temples.

fent

sent forth the most bitter lamentations. Then seized my arms, and urged my guards to vengeance. ' Perish!' cried I, ' perish! those impious wretches, ' who have violated our most sacred asylums! Arm! ' attack! destroy the inhuman monsters!' Nothing could calm my transports; till Capa-Inca, my father, informed of my fury, assured me that I should again behold thee; that you were in safety; and that we should yet enjoy each other. What new transport, what ecstacies then possessed my soul. O my dear Zilia, can the heart that has once known such plea-sure ever exist without it?

A base avidity for a despicable metal, was the sole motive that brought these barbarians to our coasts. My father knew their designs, and has prevented their demands. No sooner shall they have restored thee to my vows, than they will depart, loaded with pre-sents.—This people, whom gold has armed against us, and has made our friends, are now divested of their ferocity, and give us incessant marks of their gratitude and respect. They bow down before me, as our Cucipatas do before the Sun. Is it possible that a wretched mass of matter can thus change the heart of man; and of barbarians, as they were, make them the instruments of my felicity. Is it in the power of a metal, and of monsters, to retard, and at last to complete, our happiness.

Adorable Zilia! Light of my soul! What agita-tions has thy description of our direful separation given me? I have been present with thee in every danger. My fury was renewed: but the assurances of thy love, like a potent balm, has appealed that wound which you gave my heart. No, Zilia, life has no joy to be compared with thy love: all my powers are lost in that passion: my impatience in-creases every moment: it devours me! I burn! I die.

Zilia! give me back my life. O that Lhuama*

* The great eagle of Peru.

would

would lend you his wings—that the swiftest lightning could bear you to my arms—while my heart, yet more swiftly, flies to meet thee.

LETTER II.

To ZILIA: AZA's *despair in being deceived by the promises of the Spaniards, he flatters himself with avenging the cause of* ZILIA.

DOES this earth yet exist, O Zilia* ? Do we still behold the light of the Sun, while falsehood and treason are in his empire. Even the virtues themselves are banished from my distracted heart. Despair and fury have taken their place.

Those brutal Spaniards, who had the audacity to load thee with fetters, but were too base, too inhuman, to free thee from them, have dared to deceive me. In violation of their promises, you are not yet restored to me.

Yalpor, why dost thou withhold thy hand? Dart against these perfidious wretches, destructive thunders, like those they have purloined from thee. May some noxious flame, after a thousand torments, reduce them to ashes. . Cruel monsters! whose crime the blood of your latest posterity can alone expiate† . Perfidious nation, whose cities should be laid waste, the land sowed with stones, and deluged with blood. What horrors do you join to an infamous perjury!

Already has the sacred rays of the Sun twice enlightened his children, and my beloved Zilia is not yet restored to my impatient wishes. Those eyes, in which I ought to place my felicity, are at this mo-

---

* This letter was not sent to her.

† The Peruvians extend the punishment of crimes to the descendant of the transgressor: and where any great offence is committed, the city is treated as here described.

ment

ment drowned in floods of grief! It is, perhaps, through the moſt bitter tears thoſe fires are darted, which ought to inflame my heart. Thoſe arms in which the gods ſhould have crowned the moſt ardent love, are, perhaps, at this moment loaded with baſe fetters. O baneful grief! O diſtracting thought!

Tremble, vile mortals! The Sun has lent me his avenging powers. My injured love ſhall render them ſtill more deſtructive.

It is by thee I ſwear, thou animating fire, from whom we have received our being, and by whom we exiſt*.—It is by thy pure flames, with whoſe divine ardour I am now poſſeſſed; O Sun! may I never more behold thy genial rays: plunged in horrid night, may the pleaſing aurora never again proclaim thy return; if Aza do not deſtroy that atrocious race who have dared to pollute theſe ſacred regions with falſehood. Thou, my beloved Zilia, the unhappy object of all my tranſports, dry up thy tears. Thou ſhalt ſoon behold thy lover overthrow his enemies, break thy fetters, and caſt them on his foes. Every moment augments my fury and their puniſhment. A cruel joy is already in poſſeſſion of my heart. At this moment I ſeem to bathe in the blood of thoſe perfidious monſters. My rage is equal to my love.

I go to ſurpaſs them in barbarity: thou ſhalt be my guide; I haſte to the purſuit. Zilia, my deareſt Zilia, be aſſured of victory, for it is thy wrongs I go to avenge.

---

* The Peruvians ſuppoſe the ſoul to be an emanation from the ſun.

LETTER III.

To KANHUISCAP. *From Madrid.* AZA *deſcribes to his friend the diſtracted ſituation of his heart.*

WHAT divinity, ſenſible of my wrongs, generous friend, has preſerved thee to be the comforter of my diſtreſs ? Is it true then, that in the midſt of the moſt horrid afflictions, we can taſte ſome pleaſure ? and that how unfortunate ſoever in ourſelves, we can contribute to the happineſs of others ? Thy hands are loaded with fetters, and yet they afford me comfort : thy mind is loſt in grief, but ſtill you diminiſh my infelicity.

A ſtranger, and a captive, in theſe barbarous regions, you make me ſtill enjoy my country, though ſo far diſtant from it. Dead to the reſt of mankind, I would live alone for you. It is only to you that my diſtracted mind is able to expreſs itſelf, and that my feeble hands can ſometimes form thoſe knots which unite us in defiance of our cruel enemies.

You will forgive me, if the moſt tender and ardent love does more frequently preſent itſelf, than friendſhip and revenge. The pleaſures of the one are a conſolation, the violence of the other has its charms : but all things yield to love. It is not, that ſubdued by the ſtrokes of fortune, my afflictions have diminiſhed my courage. A king, I think as a king : though a ſlave, I ſuffer no ſentiments of ſlavery to approach me. I thirſt for vengeance, though without hope. Fain would I change both thy lot and my own. Alas ! I can only deplore them.

From our native land we were tranſported to a new world ; and in ſpite of my prayers, we were ſeparated. Our friendſhip became an object of fear to our conquerors : accuſtomed to crimes, could they do otherwiſe than dread our virtues ? Was it thus, Kanhuiſcap,
that

that the day fhould have ended, on which thy courage
and mine, and, what is more, my love, ought to have
rendered me, by victory, worthy of the power that
had armed me; of that bright ftar which gave me
birth; and worthy of thy applaufe: when the Sun,
the foe to perjury, fhould have avenged his children;
fhould have feafted them with the fmoking flefh of
thofe deteftable monfters, and have drenched them
with their blood?

Is it thus that I muft revenge the wrongs of Zilia?
while fhe, confumed by the moft ardent love, ftill burns
in thofe fetters which I cannot break. Zilia! whom
the infamous ravifhers . . . . . O ye gods, hide from
me thofe dreadful images . . . . . What do I fay, Kanhuifcap, the gods themfelves cannot banifh them
from my mind. I can no longer behold my Zilia; a
cruel element divides us. Perhaps her griefs . . . . our
enemies . . . . the waves . . . . . . a mortal ftroke now
pierces my heart. My friend! I fink under the weight
of my diftrefs. My quipos fall from my hands.
Zilia . . . . . my beloved Zilia!

LETTER IV.

To the fame: alarms of AZA *for the fate of* ZILIA*; of
whom he has had frightful prefages.*

FAITHFUL Anqui, thy quipos have a moment
fufpended my alarms, but they cannot difperfe them.
To that healing balm which thy friendfhip fpreads
over my woes, conftantly fucceeds a dreadful remembrance. At every inftant I fee my Zilia in fetters;
the Sun difgraced; his temples profaned: I behold my
father bending under the weight of chains, as well as
years: I fee my country defolated. I exift by miferies
alone; and every circumftance ferves to increafe them.
The fhades of the night prefent me with nought but
frightful images. In vain do I feek tranquillity in
the

the arms of sleep; there I find nothing but torments.
This very night Zilia again prefented herfelf before
me. The horrors of death were painted on her countenance. My name feemed to efcape from her dying
lips: I faw it traced on the quipos that fell from her
hands. Unknown barbarians, their arms ftained with
blood, in the midft of flames and tumult, took her
from one of thofe enormous machines in which we
were tranfported. They feemed to prefent her in triumph to their hideous chief: when, in an inftant,
the fea mounting to the clouds, offered nothing to my
fight but waves of blood, floating carcafes, large logs
of wood partly confumed, fires, and devouring flames.
In vain would I diffipate thefe melancholy ideas; they
continually return, and fix themfelves in my mind.
Nothing alleviates my diftrefs: every thing augments
it. I hate even the air I breathe. I reproach the
waves with not having fwallowed me up. I complain
to the gods that they ftill fuffer me to exift. If their
bounty, lefs cruel, permitted me to forfake this light;
if I could difpofe of this fpark of divinity which they
have communicated to me; if it were not a horrible
crime for a mortal to deftroy the work of the divinity;
could my weaknefs be condemned, Kanhuifcap?
Ought my fpirit to wander in the air? My miferies
would have an end. But what do I fay? Each day
increafes them. Participate with me, O Kanhuifcap! my piercing griefs: learn, if it be poffible,
fome news of Zilia; while my diftracted heart demands
her of the gods—of all nature—of myfelf.

LETTER.

LETTER V.

To the fame: AZA *conceives hope of receiving from* KANHUISCAP *fome account of* ZILIA.

MAY thofe divine rays which give us life, comfort thee with their moft benignant warmth. Kanhuif-cap, thou haft kindled in my heart the moft flattering hopes. The progrefs you have made in the Spanifh language has already enabled you to learn, that the firft veffels which were expected to arrive on the coaft where you dwell, will come from the empire of the Sun. By them you will know the fate of her for whom alone I exift. Judge therefore with what im-pat'ence I attend your informations. I already launch forth into the regions of happinefs. The fituation of Zilia is laid open to my fight. Already do I fee her reftored to the temple of the Sun; void of all grief but that of my diftance from her. There fhe decks the altars of the god, and adorns them as much by her charms as by the works of her hands. As fome beauteous flower after a ftorm, but ftill agitated by the winds, receives the frefh rays of the fun, while the water that covers it ferves only to augment its luftre; fo does Zilia feem more blooming, and more dear to my heart. Now fhe appears to me like the fun after a long obfcurity, whofe bright beams dazzle the fight, and declares the return of a pleafing feafon. Then I feem to be at her feet. There I experience concern, emotion, pleafure, refpect, tendernefs, and all thofe fentiments with which I was affected, when in reality I enjoyed her prefence. Even thofe, Kan-huifcap, with which her heart was agitated, I then prove. How ftrong are the chains of illufion! but yet how delightful! My real evils are deftroyed by ima-ginary pleafures. I behold Zilia happy; and my feli-city is complete.

O my

O my dear Kanhuilcap, do not fruftrate a hope in which my happinefs confifts, and which may be deftroyed by impatience alone. Do not let the leaft retardment, my generous friend, delay my happinefs. May thy quipos, knotted by the hands of gladnefs, be borne to me upon the wings of the wind; and in return for thy friendfhip, may the moft exquifite perfumes be continually diffufed over thy head.

LETTER VI.

To the fame : the inquietudes of AZA *are calmed by the news which his friend gives him of* ZILIA.

OF what delicious waters haft thou made ufe, my dear friend, to quench that cruel fire which devoured my heart? To inquietudes that diftracted me unceafingly, and to griefs by which I was totally overwhelmed, you have made to fucceed tranquillity and joy. I foon fhall again behold my Zilia. O happinefs almoft unhoped for! But yet fhe is withheld from me. O cruel procraftination! In vain does my heart go forth to meet her. In vain does my whole foul attempt to mix with her's; there is ftill enough left to tell me that I am far from her.

Soon fhall I again behold her; and that delightful thought, far from calming, increafes, my inquietude. —Separated from my life itfelf, judge what torments I endure. At each moment I die; and recover but to defire in vain. Like the hunter who in running to quench, augments, the thirft that devours him, fo does my hope render more fierce the flame that confumes me. The nearer I approach to an union with Zilia, the more I fear to lofe her. How often, my faithful friend, has one moment already feparated us; and that cruel moment, at the height of my felicity, I ftill fear.

O An

An element, cruel as inconltant, is the depofitory of
my happinels.   Say you not, that Zilia abandons the
empire of the Sun, to come to thefe horrid climates?
A long time wandering on the fea before fhe can reach
thefe coafts, what dangers has fhe not to experience!
And how much more have I not to fear for her! But
whither does my paffion carry me? I am talking of
mifery, when all things promife happinels; joys of
which the thought alone! . . . . . Ah! Kanhuilcap,
what tranfports, what feelings, hitherto unknown!
Every fenfe feparately enjoys the fame pleafure—Zilia
is before my eyes.   I hear the tender accents of her
voice.   I embrace her: I die.

LETTER VII.

*To the fame: AZA with ALONZO, who inflructs him
in the manners of the Spaniards.*

AS fubject to viciffitude, as accident can prevent my
felicity, Kanhuilcap, fo the term to which you refer
its completion muft neceffarily diminifh it.

Before the Sun can make me happy, he muft a hundred times enlighten the world! Before that immenfity
of time, Zilia cannot be reftored to me.

In vain does friendfhip endeavour to foften the
rigours of my lot: it can by no means diveft me of
anxiety.

Alonzo, whom the unjuft Capa-Inca of the Spaniards has appointed to fit, with my father, on the
throne of the Sun: Alonzo, to whom the Spaniards
have given me in charge, in vain attempts to free me
from my diftrefs.   The friendfhip which he fhews me;
the cuftoms of his countrymen which he points out
to me; the amufements that he endeavours to procure
me; the reflections to which I abandon myfelf, are
not able to make me forget my misfortunes.

'I hat

That piercing grief into which the feparation from
Zilia had thrown me, has hitherto prevented me from
giving any attention to the objects that furround me.
I faw, I breathed, nothing but mifery. I feemed to
find pleafure, fo to fay, in my misfortunes: fcarcely
could I be faid to live. how then could I form reflections? But no fooner had I given to joy thofe moments that love affigned it, than I began to open my
eyes. What objects then ftruck my fight! I cannot
defcribe to you how much they yet furprife me. I
found myfelf alone, in the midft of a world that I
never thought had exifted. I there faw beings whom
whom I refemble. We each appeared to be feized
with an equal furprife: my eager looks were loft in
their's. A numberlefs people are continually agitated
in the fame circle, and in which they feem to be confined. Others that are feldom feen, and who are diftinguifhed from the former by their idlenefs alone.
Tumults, cries, quarrels, combats, a frightful uproar, and one continued confufion. This, at firft, was
all that I could difcern.

At the beginning my mind, embracing too many
objects, could not diftinguifh any one of them. It
was not long before I was fenfible of this; I therefore determined to prefcribe bounds to my obfervations, and to begin with reflecting on thofe objects that
were neareft to me : the houfe of Alonzo therefore is
become the centre of my thoughts. The Spaniards
I there fee feem to be fubjects fufficient to employ me
for a long time ; and by their difpofitions I fhall be
enabled to judge of their fellow-countrymen. Alonzo,
who has dwelt a confiderable time in our country, and
confequently is converfant in our language and cuftoms, aids me in the difcoveries I would make. This
fincere friend, uninfected with the prejudices of his
countrymen, frequently points out to me the ridiculous part of their conduct. ' Behold that grave man,'
faid he to me, the other day, ' who by his haughty
' mien, his curled muftaches, his high-crowned cap,

' and-

‘ and numerous train, you would take for another
‘ Huayna Capac*; but he is a Cucipata, who has
‘ sworn to our Pachacamac to be humble, meek, and
‘ poor.　He that you saw drink those large draughts
‘ of liquors, that have left him scarce any remains of
‘ reason, is a judge; who, within an hour, is to de-
‘ cide on the lives or fortunes of a number of citizens.
‘ That man you see who is more amorous of himself,
‘ than of the lady to whom he seems to pay so much
‘ regard : he who can scarcely support the heat of the
‘ weather, and of that perfumed habit which he
‘ wears : who talks with so much emotion on the least
‘ trifle : whose debaucheries have sunk his eyes, paled
‘ his visage, and even destroyed his voice ; that is a
‘ general, who is to lead thirty thousand men to
‘ battle.’

It is thus, Kanhuiscap, by the aid of Alonzo, that
I dissipate, for some moments, the anxieties that con-
sume me.　But, alas! they soon return : for the
amusements of the mind must for ever give place to
the affections of the heart.

LETTER VIII.

To the same :　Aza paints to his friend the character of
ALONZO.

THE observations which Alonzo has enabled me to
make of the characters of his countrymen, have not
prevented me from sometimes reflecting on his own.
Though I am an admirer of the virtues of this sincere
friend, I do not forbear to remark his defects.　Wise,
generous, and brave, he is notwithstanding weak, and
subject to those very follies he condemns.　‘ Behold
‘ that respectable and dreadful warrior,’ he said, ‘ that
‘ firm defender of our country, that man who by a
‘ single glance of his eye can make thousands obey

* The name of the great conqueror of Peru.

　　　　　　　　　　　　　　　‘ him :

'him: yet he is a flave in his own houfe, and fubject
'to every little caprice of his wife.' So does Alonzo
appear to me when his daughter, Zulmira, enters.
From the imperious air fhe conftantly affects when
her father tenderly embraces her, I am convinced that
Alonzo is, with regard to his daughter, what the
warrior is to his wife: and do not imagine that he is
the only Spaniard who does not fpare in others the
faults of which he is himfelf guilty. I was walking
the other day in a public garden, where I diftinguifhed among the crowd, a little monfter, about the fize of
a Vicuna*, his legs were contorted like the Amaruc†,
and his head fo funk between his fhoulders, that
fcarcely could he move it. I could not reftrain from
commiferating the lot of this unfortunate creature,
when I was furprifed by loud peals of laughter. I
turned toward the part from whence they came. But
what was my furprife! when I found they were caufed
by a man, almoft as deformed as the other, and who
was pointing out to the company, the difertions of
his brother. Is it poffible we can be fo blind to our
own faults, when we are fo fenfible of them in others?
Does the excefs of virtue then become a vice?

Alonzo, though fubject to his daughter, would be
inexcufable not to love her. The vivacity of her wit,
the beauty and the graces which the Creator has given
her: her ftately port, and the tender language of her
eyes, in fpite of the fire with which they fparkle;
convince me that fhe has a heart fenfible, but vain;
that fhe is tender, but impetuous, even in the moft
trifling purfuits. What a difference, my dear friend,
between her and Zilia! Zilia, who almoft infenfible to
her beauty, would hide it from every one but her conqueror: fhe who is conducted by candour and modefty, and whofe heart, the pureft and moft tender love
alone poffeffes; in whom the movements of pride have
no place, who defpifes all the turns of art; fhe who
knows of no means to pleafe but by love; fhe who . . . . .

* A kind of Indian goat.   † The adder of the Indians.

Ah! how fierce the flame that now confumes my heart? Zilia? my beloved Zilia! Shall I never again behold thee? What can yet retaid our felicity? Are the gods themfelves jealous of the happine⟨s of a mortal? O my dear friend, if it be to them alone that belong the joys of love, why are we made fenfible to the power of beauty? Or why, when mafters of our hearts, do they fuffer us to afpire after a happinefs, which they are unwilling we fhall poffefs?

LETTER IX.

To the fame: the manners and cuftoms of the Spaniards are totally different in their own country from what they are in Mexico.

WITHOUT the affiftance of the Spanifh language, the reflections which Alonzo communicates to me could not extend beyond certain bounds, and thofe which I made myfelf could be but fuperficial. Defirous of diverting my impatience, I have fought a mafter who could inftruct me in this language. The informations he has given me, have already enabled me to profit by converfation, and examine more nearly, the genius and tafte of a people who feem to have be n created folely for the deftruction of mankind; of whom, however, they appear to think themfelves the ornament. At firft I imagined that thefe ambitious barbarians, who employ themfelves in contriving miferies for nations of whom they are ignorant; drank nothing but blood: beheld the Sun through a thick fmoke only, and were folely employed in forging inftruments of death: for you know (as well as myfelf) that the thunder with which they fmote us, was formed by them. I expected to have found in their cities nothing but makers of thunder: foldiers exercifing in the courfe, or combat: princes ftained with the blood they had fhed, and braving, in order to enable them

to

to fhed more, the heats of the day, the rigours of winter, fatigue, and death itfelf.

You will eafily conceive my furprife, when inftead of that theatre of blood which I had formed in my imagination, I here found the throne of mercy. This people, who, I believe, are cruel towards us only, appear to be governed by benevolence. The inhabitants feem to be united by a clofe friendfhip. They never meet without giving marks of efteem, amity, and even of refpect. Thefe fentiments fparkle in their eyes, and govern their bodies. They bow down before each other. In a word, by their continual embraces, they appear to be rather one family, happily united, than a collection of people. Thofe warriors, who to us appeared fo formidable, are here no other than old men, who are ftill more amiable than the reft; or youths, gay, gentle, and officious to pleafe. That urbanity which governs them, that eafe with which they perform all their actions, thofe pleafures which are their only ftudies, and thofe fentiments of humanity which they difcover, induces me to think that they have two fouls, one for fociety, the other for war.

In fact, what a difference! You have feen them, my friend, bring within our walls defolation, horror, and death. The groans of our women expiring by their wounds; the venerable age of our fathers, the piercing cries fent forth by the tender organs of our children, the majefty of our temples, the facred awe that furrounds them; all things ferved to augment their barbarity.

And now I behold them adoring thofe virtues they then deftroyed: giving honour to age: ftretching forth a benignant hand to infancy, and venerating the temples they profaned; can thefe therefore be the fame men?

LETTER

LETTER X.

To the same: Aza's reflections on the diverfity of tafte among the Spaniards.

THE more I reflect on the variety of difpofitions among the Spaniards, the lefs able am I to determine the principle from which they proceed. This nation feems to have but one that is general, and it is that which leads to idlenefs. There is here, however, a divinity that nearly refembles it, and that is called Tafte. A large felect number of adorers facrifice all things to this; even their tranquillity. There is, however, a party (and that party is the moft fincere) who acknowledge that they know not who this is. The others, more prefuming, give definitions of it, which are as unintelligible to themfelves as to the reft of mankind. According to many, it is a divinity that is not the lefs real for being invifible. Every one ought to feel its infpirations. We are to agree with the fculpture, that it is concealed under a figure of a hideous fhape, which appears to flutter with the two wings of a bat, and which an infant holds elegantly enchained with a garland of flowers. One of thofe fort of men, whom they call here *petit-maitres*, will oblige you to believe that this divinity is to be found in his waiftcoat, and not in that of his companion, and the proof he brings (which you cannot refute) is that the buttonholes of his waiftcoat are either greater or lefs than thofe of the other.

Some days fince I faw an edifice of which I had heard very unintelligible accounts. When I approached it, I found at the gate two troops of Spaniards, who feemed to be at open war with each other. I afked of one who accompanied me, what was the caufe of their contention. ' It is,' he replied, ' a matter of great ' confequence'. They are about to determine the re-
' putation

' putation of this temple, and the rank it shall hold
' with posterity. These people you here see are con-
' noisseurs. The one side asserts, that it is a mere
' heap of stones, remarkable for nothing but its enor-
' mity. The other maintains that it is by no means
' enormous, but is constructed in true taste.'

Leaving those connoisseurs, I entered the temple. I
had gone but a few paces, when I saw painted against
the wall, the figure of a venerable old man, the sere-
nity and dignity of whose features inspired respect.
He appeared to be borne upon the winds, and was
surrounded by winged infants whose eyes were directed to the earth. ' Whom does that picture re-
' present?' I said. ' It is,' replied an old Cucipatas,
after several inclinations of his body, ' the represen-
' tation of the Lord of the universe, who by the
' breath of his nostrils, produced all things out of
' nothing. But have you examined,' he cried with
precipitation, ' those precious stones which cover this
' altar?' He had scarcely finished those words, when
the beauty of one of those diamonds had struck me.
It represented a man whose head was incircled with
laurels. I immediately asked who the man was, that
had merited a place by the side of the Creator. ' It
' is,' replied the Cucipatas with a smile, ' the head
' of the most cruel and most despicable prince that
' ever existed.' That answer threw me into a series
of reflections which the want of expressions prevents
me from communicating. When I had recovered
from my first astonishment, with respectful steps I was
quitting the temple, when another object struck me.
In an obscure place I discovered, amidst the dust, the
head of an old man who had neither the majesty nor
the benignity of the other. But what was my astonishment, when they would have persuaded me that it
was the portrait of the same divinity, the Creator of
all things. The little respect which the Cucipatas
appeared to have for this head prevented me from believing it, and I came away, offended with the impo-
sition.

fition. For in fact, what appearance is there, Kan-huifcap, that the fame men, in the fame place, fhould adore a God, and tread him under their feet.

This is not the only contradiction that is to be found among the Spaniards. Nothing is more common than thofe inconfiftencies which time produces in this country. Why do they deftroy that palace, whofe folidity promifes at leaft another century of duration? 'Becaufe,' they reply, 'it is not in 'tafte. When firft erected, it was confidered as a 'chef d'œuvre, and was built at a great expence. 'But in thefe days it appears ridiculous.'

Though this nation is fo much a flave to this pretended tafte, yet it is not neceffary that every particular perfon have it. There are here people of tafte, who fell it dearly to thofe who by caprice imagine them to be in poffeffion of it. Alonzo made me remark, the other day, one of thofe men who have the reputation of dreffing themfelves with a certain elegance, in which, according to him, they place great merit. As a contraft to that man, he fhewed me at the fame time another who was regarded as having no tafte. I am unable to decide between them, feeing the public, before whom they appear, agrees in laughing at both of them. From whence the only real difference that I can difcover between him who has tafte, and him who has none, is, that they both depart from nature, but by different ways; and that the god they call Tafte, fixes his abode fometimes at the end of one of thefe paths, and fometimes at that of the other. Unhappy therefore is the man who takes the wrong path: he is difgraced and defpifed; till the god, changing his abode at the moment he leaft thinks of it, puts it in his power to treat others with equal feverity.

However, Kanhuifcap, if you will believe the Spaniards, nothing is more invariable than tafte, and the reafon of its having fo often changed, is becaufe their anceftors were ignorant of that in which it truly confifts.

ſtr. But much I fear that the ſame reproach will be made by their lateſt poſterity.

LETTER XI.

To the ſame: Aza *continues his reflections on the vices of the Spaniards.*

CAN I expreſs my ſurpriſe, Kanhuiſcap, when I find that in this country, which I imagined to have been inhabited by virtue itſelf, it is only by force that men are here virtuous. It is the fear of puniſhment and of death, that alone inſpires men here with thoſe ſentiments that I thought nature had engraved in their hearts. There are, in this country, whole volumes, which are filled with the prohibitions of vice. There is no crime ſo horrid but what has here its proper puniſhment aſſigned it; nay, that has not an example. In fact, it was not ſo much a wiſe precaution, as the models of vices, that have dictated the decrees by which they are prohibited. To judge by theſe laws, what crimes are there that the Spaniards have not committed? They have a God, and have blaſphemed him; a king, and have rebelled againſt him; a faith which they have violated. They love and reſpect, yet murder, each other. They are friends, yet betray; they are united by religion, yet deteſt their brethren. Where then, I am continually aſking myſelf, is that union which I at firſt remarked among this people? That pleaſing chain by-which friendſhip ſeemed to have united their hearts? Can I imagine that it was formed of nothing but fear or intereſt? But what I find moſt aſtoniſhing, is the continuance of theſe laws. What? can a people who have violated the moſt ſacred laws of nature, and have ſtifled her voice, ſuffer themſelves to be governed by the feeble voice of their anceſtors? Can this people, like their Hamas, open the mouth to a bit, which is

cauſed

offered them by a man whose equal they have already
destroyed! Ah! Karhuilcap, how unhappy is the
prince who reigns over such a people! How many
snares has he to avoid? If he would preserve his authority, he must be virtuous; yet he has constantly
vice before his eyes: Perjury surrounds him; Pride
goes before him; Perfidy, with downcast looks, follows his footsteps; and never can he behold Truth,
but by the false glare of the torch of Envy.

Such is the true picture of that throng which surrounds the prince, and which they call the court.
The nearer we approach the throne, the further we
recede from virtue. We there see a vile flatterer by
the side of the defender of his country; a buffoon
linked with the most consummate minister; perjury,
escaped from its just punishment, there usurps the
rank of probity. Yet from the midst of this crowd of
criminals. it is, that the king pronounces justice.
There it should seem as if the laws are only taught by
those who are the violaters. The judgment that condemns one criminal, is frequently signed by another.
For how rigorous soever these laws may be, they are
not made for every one. In the closet of the judge a
fine woman in tears falling at his feet; or a man who
brings with him a considerable quantity of pieces of
gold; easily exculpates the most atrocious criminal,
while the innocent expire in tortures! O Kanhuilcap!
how happy are the children of the Sun, who are guided
by rectitude alone! Ignorant of vice, they fear no
punishment; and as Virtue is their judge, Nature is
their law.

LETTER XII.

To the same: continuation of the same subject.

I T rarely happens, that the first point of view from which we behold any object, is that from which it appears in the truest light. What difference, Kanhuiscap, between this people and those I thought I first saw. All their virtue is nothing but a slender veil, through which we distinguish the features of those who would screen themselves from our view. Under the dazzling éclat of the most virtuous actions, you may constantly discern the seeds of some vice. Like the rays of the sun, which, while they seem to give a lustre to the colour of the rose, discover the thorns that are hidden beneath it. An insupportable pride is the source of that amiable union with which I was at first so highly charmed. The tender embrace, the affected respect, proceed from the same source. The least infliction of the body is here regarded as an acknowledgment that is due to rank or friendship. The most detestable characters in the nation, and they who have the greatest aversion, mutually render each other this idle homage. A great man passes by you, and uncovers his head; that is an honour: he smiles upon you; that is a favour. But it is not remembered, that the purchase of this honourable salute, and of this flattering smile, is attended with a thousand submissions and mortifications. To speak more justly, in order to obtain these honours, it is necessary to become a slave.

Pride has still another veil, and that is gravity: that varnish which gives an air of reason to the most senseless actions. He who, though possessed of great wit and sense, is regarded as a tool, would have been held in the highest esteem, though totally destitute of both those accomplishments, if he had but concealed

P   cealed

cealed his love of pleasure. To be wise is nothing; the only thing necessary is to appear so.

' That man, whose sagacity and accomplishments ' correspond with the benignity of his countenance,' said Alonzo the other day! ' that man of an almost ' universal genius, has been excluded from the most ' important employments, for having once laughed in- ' considerately!' You will not therefore be surprised, Kanhuiscap, that they here perform actions in them- selves the most sottish, with the utmost solemnity. This affected gravity, however, makes no great impression on me. I perceive the pride of him by whom it is used, and the more he esteems himself, the more I despise him. Are merit and mirth by nature antipathies? No; for reason never suffers by those pleasures which the mind alone enjoys.

LETTER XIII.

To the same: AZA *describes his embarrassment and imperfect ideas concerning the doctrines of the Christian religion.*

I CANNOT avoid again repeating to you, Kanhuis- cap, that there seems to me to be something unde- finable in the character of the Spaniards. Every day produces some fresh contradiction. What do you think, for example, of the following? This people have a divinity whom they adore * : but far from mak- ing him any offerings, it is their God who nourishes them. You see in their temples no Curaccas †, as

---

* We must remember here, that it is a Peruvian who speaks, and one who has but a very imperfect notion of our religion.

† These Curaccas were statues, of different metals, and in different habits, which they placed in their temples; and were as it were so many, to express the several wants of those that of- fered them.

fymbols of their wants. In a word, there are certain times of the day, when you would take thefe temples for deferted palaces.

Certain ancient women, however, remain there almoft the whole day. The air of devotion which they affect, and the tears which they fhed, attracted at firft my regard; and the difdain with which they were treated, excited my compaffion; till I was undeceived by Alonzo, ' Thofe women,' faid he, ' who have ac- ' quired your efteem, are but little known to you. ' One of thofe you fee is paid by proftitutes, to procure ' them traffic for their charms. That other facrifices ' her fortune and her repofe to the deftruction of her ' family.'

Unnatural mothers truft their children to thofe they would not truft a trifling jewel, in order to come here and adore a God, who, according to their own confeffion, has given them no ftronger commandment than that of properly educating thofe children. Others, having forfaken the pleafures of the world becaufe they can no longer enjoy them, here make a virtue of depreciating vices which they have obferved in other finners.

How difficult are thefe barbarous nations, Kanhuifcap, to reconcile with themfelves. Their religion is not more difficult to reconcile with that of nature. They acknowledge, with us, a God, the creator, who differs, it is true, from our's, as he is entirely a pure fubftance; or, to fpeak more properly, an affemblage of all perfections. No limits can be prefcribed to his power: his being can fuffer no variation. Wifdom, juftice, and mercy, omnipotence and immutability, compofe his effence. This God has ever exifted, and for ever will exift. Such is the definition which one of the Cucipatas of this empire has given me: for they are ignorant of nothing that has happened fince, nor even before, the creation of the world. It was this God who placed mankind upon the earth, as in garden of pleafure: but they were foon plunged into the abyfs

P 2   of

of pains and miferies ; after which they were deftroyed.
One man, however, was exempted from this general
deftruction, and repeopled the earth—with men ftill
more wicked than the former. God, notwithftanding,
far from punifhing them, chofe from among them a
certain number, to whom he dictated his laws, and
promifed to fend his Son. But this ungrateful people,
forgetting the goodnefs of God, facrificed his Son, the
moft dear pledge of his paternal tendernefs. Rendered by this crime the object of God's hatred, that nation was vifited by his vengeance. Wandering inceffantly from country to country, the whole univerfe
was a witnefs of their chaftifement. It was on other
men, until that time lefs worthy of the divine favour,
that the Son, fo long promifed, beftowed his munifi-
cence. It was for them that he inftituted new laws,
which differed but in few things from thofe that
were before.

Such, my fagacious friend, was the conduct of their
God towards mankind. Now, how will you reconcile
this with his effence * ? He is almighty and immutable.
He created thefe people to make them happy : and yet
they were not rendered by any means free from the
infirmities of human nature. He would have them
happy, yet their laws forbid them that pleafure which
he made for them, as they for pleafure. He is juft,
and does not punifh in the children thofe crimes which
he has fo feverely punifhed in the fathers. He is merci-
ful, and his clemency is not fooner exhaufted than his
feverity. Perfuaded as they are of the goodnefs, wifdom, and power of God, you will perhaps imagine,
Kanhuifcap, that the Spaniards are faithful to his
laws, and follow them with precifion : but if you
think fo, your error is great. Abandoned inceffantly,
and without referve, to vices prohibited by his
laws, they prove, that either the juftice of God is

* We fhall ftill remember, that it is an unlearned *Peruvian*
who fpeaks.

not

not fufficiently fevere; that he does not punifh thofe
actions which he forbids: or that his laws are too
rigid, as they prohibit thofe actions which his goodnefs
prevents him from punifhing.

LETTER XXI.

To the fame: ZILIA *is continually prefent to the mind
of* AZA, *in the midft of all his reflections. An account of the intrigues and hypocrify of the Spanifh women.*

PERHPAS you have thought, my faithful friend,
that, foftened by time, the impatience which devoured
my heart began to be exhaufted.   I pardon thy error;
for myfelf have been the caufe of it.   The reflections
you have feen me give myfelf up to, for fome time paft,
could not proceed, as you thought, but from a heart
that was at eafe.   No longer perfift in an error that is
injurious to me.   Impatience frequently borrows from
a feeming tranquillity the moft cruel arms.   This I
have but too much experienced.   My mind contem-
plated, with a wandering eye, the different objects
that prefented themfelves: my heart was not the lefs
devoured by impatience.   Conftantly prefented to my
fight, Zilia perpetuated my anxiety, even in thofe moments when my philofophy feemed to you to fe-
cure my tranquillity.   An application to the fciences may divert, but it can never make us forget,
our paffions: and even if it had that power, what
could it effect on an inclination that is founded on reafon?   My love, you know, is not one of thofe tranfient
vapours which, raifed by caprice, are foon diffipated.
Reafon, that taught me to know my heart, told me
that it was made for love.   It was by the light of his
torch I firft perceived I loved.   Could I refrain from
following his fteps?   He fhewed me beauty in the eyes
of Zilia: he made me feel its power, her charms, and
my felicity; and, far from oppofing my happinefs, rea-

fon taught me that it frequently alone confifted in the art of raifing and preferving pleafures. You will judge then, Karhuiscap, if philofophy has been able to diminifh my love. The reflections I have made on the Spanifh women cannot but increafe it. That great difparity of virtue, of beauty, and of fentiment, which I have remarked between them and Zilia, makes me more fenfible of my mifery in being feparated from her. That pure candour, that amiable freedom, thofe foft tranfports in which her foul delights, are here mere veils to cover licentioufnefs and perfidy. To conceal the moft ardent paffion, in order to difplay one that they did not feel, far from being punifhed as a vice, is here regarded as an accomplifhment. To attempt to pleafe any particular perfon is a crime; not to pleafe all is a difgrace. Such are the principles of virtue that they here engrave on the hearts of their women. When any one of them has the happinais, if it be a happinefs, to be efteemed beautiful, fhe muft prepare to receive the homage of a crowd of adorers, whofe worfhip fhe is to reward, by at leaft one glance of the eye each day. When a woman of this fort is what they call a *coquette*, the firft ftep fhe takes is to find out among the crowd, him who is the moft opulent. This difcovery being made, all her actions, all her arts tend to captivate him: fhe fucceeds, and marries him: then fhe confuls her heart. Her beauty now is employed to another purpofe; fhe gces daily to the temples, and to the public places: there, through a veil that prevents her blufhes, fhe regards, with a fteady eye, the faithful troop that pafs before her. Alvarez and Pedro foon divide her heart. She balances between them, and decides for the former; but concealing her choice from both, leaves them to figh. Without difcouraging Pedro, fhe makes Alvarez happy: grows tired of him, and returns to Pedro, whom fhe foon abandons for another. This is not the moft difficult of her enterprifes. She is to perfuade all the world that fhe

loves

loves her hufband, and to convince him of his happinefs, in having a wife who fcrupuloufly performs
her duty. The public has alfo a duty to perform,
which it does with great punctuality; and that is to
remind the hufband that he is married to a *fine* woman. Thefe contagious examples appear to have extended even to Zulmira, whofe heart they have in-
fected. I think I difcover, that, though yet a ch'ld,
fhe is poffeffed with the dangerous paffion of defiring
to pleafe. Every trifling action, her moft indifferent
regards, have conftantly fomething that feems to come
from her heart. Her flattering difcourfes, her ex-
preffive looks, the affecting tone of her voice, which
is frequently loft in tender fighs, all declare it. Thus
it is, Kanhuifcap, that by differe t arts, virtue here
has frequently the outward app-arance of vice, while
vice is concealed under the maik of virtue.

LETTER XV.

To the fame : AZA, *better inftructed in the nature of
the ftars, and of thunder, is difgufted of the ancient
prejudices of his nation.*

O THAT truth at which I am ftill aftonifhed! O
amazing depth of knowledge! Kanhuifcap, the fun,
that mafter-piece of nature, the earth, the prolific fea,
are not gods. A Creator, different from our's, has
produced them; and by a fingle look he can deftroy
them. From the midft of a vaft chaos, enveloped by
lifelefs matter, from the bofom of confufion, he called
forth the refplendent ftars, and the people who adore
them. To every part of matter he gave a productive
virtue. The fun, at his voice, poured forth its light;
the moon received its rays, and tranfmitted them to
us. The earth produced, and nourifhed by its juices,
thofe trees, thofe animals which we adore. The fea,
which a God alone could rule, affords us fuftenance
by

by the fishes it contains: and man, created master of
the universe, reigns over all other creatures. It was
the ignorance of those mysteries, my dear friend, that
has caused all our misfortunes. Had we been instructed, like the Spaniards, in the secret of nature,
we should have known, that the thunder they darted
on us was nothing but a mass of matter which is to
be found in our own country: that Yalpor himself,
that terrible god, is no more than a vapour which
the earth produces, and whose course is directed by
chance: that those furious Hamas, which fly before
us, we might make subservient to our use: had we
known these things, could we have calmly reflected on
the dignity of our ancestors, and suffered ourselves to
serve as a triumph to these barbarians? In effect,
Kanhuilcap, it seems as if nature stood full exposed
before their eyes. Her most secret actions are known
to them. They discover what is doing in the highest
heavens, and in the most profound abyss. It seems,
moreover, as if it were no longer in the power of nature to change what they have once foreseen.

LETTER XVI.

*To the same: account of the hypocritic and superstitious
practices in religion among the Spaniards. Judicious
reflections of AZA on the Auto de Fè.*

COULD I have imagined, Kanhuilcap, that this
people, who seem to enjoy the light of reason in its
highest perfection, should be slaves to the opinions of
their ancestors? How false soever it may be, a notion
once received must here be constantly followed: it cannot be controverted without a risk of being taxed, at
least, with singularity. The judgment of nature, her
voice so distinct, which we incessantly hear, is drowned; her blazing torch is extinguished by prejudice: a
tyrant, who, though hated, is nevertheless powerful;
a cheat,

Publiſhed by P. Kirk.   PERUVIAN PRINCESS.   Engraved by . Warren.

Vide Vol II Letter 21 page 157

Alonzo entreating ..za to quit the gloomy ſcenes
he frequented to indulge his grief for the loſs of Z..a.

Engraved As C divke March 8 1797

THE PERUVIAN PRINCESS.   157

a cheat, who, though well known, is, notwithftanding, dangerous. This tyrant, however, might eafily
be overcome, if he were not allied with one ftill more
potent than himfelf; that is, fuperftition. It is by
this falfe light that moft men are here guided, and
which makes them miftake fabulous accounts for real
matters of fact. A man who frequents the temples
feveral times a day, who appears with a hypocritical
and diftorted countenance, what vice foever he may be
a flave to, or whatever crimes he may commit, will
be generally efteemed ; while the moft virtuous, if he
throw off the yoke of prejudice, will be treated with
contempt. The man void of prejudice, is here faid
to be void of piety. It is not fufficient to be what
is called wife; to this muft be added the title of devout, or elfe you muft expect that of profligate. The
difpenfers of the public efteem, thofe men who are fo
defpicable in themfelves, will never admit of an inter-
mediate clafs. To be neither devout nor libertine,
is to them a paradox. Such a man appears to their
deluded fight like an amphibious monfter. The Spaniards have two divinities, one who prefides over virtue, and the other over vice. If, without affectation,
you content yourfelf with facrificing to the former
only, you will foon be taxed with being a worfhipper
of the latter. The empire of virtue is by no means
abfolute; its fubjects have much to fear from the divinity of vice. They are conftantly obliged to appear in public with arms proper to encounter him,
and with which, however, they are not always able
to defend themfelves. They feized, the other day,
a man who had committed many crimes, and they
publicly declared that the devil muft have led him to
that excefs of abomination. He had, however, about
his neck a fort of cord that had been confecrated by
the Cucipatas of the God of Virtue. In one hand
he held another cord, on which were ftrung a number
of beads, that had the power of driving away the
author of his crimes; and in the other the dagger
with

with which he had committed them. I was yesterday carried to a spacious place, where a prodigious number of people expressed the highest joy, on beholding several of their fellow-mortals burned to death. The strange habits in which they were dressed, and that air of satisfaction which appeared in the sacrificers, as if at a triumph, made me take them for victims that those savages were offering to their gods. But what was my astonishment, when I learned that the God of these barbarians beholds the shedding of blood, not only of men, but of beasts, with abhorrence! With what horror was I seized, when I reflected that it was to the God of mercy these licentious priests made those detested offerings. Can these Cucipatas mean to appease their divinity by such sacrifices? Must not the expiation be even more offensive to him than the crimes of the offenders? Ah, Kanhuiscap, how deplorable an error!

LETTER XVII.

To the same: Aza communicates to his friend his ideas relative to the philosophic knowledge he had acquired.

THE desire of information you appear to have, my faithful friend, at once pleases and perplexes me. You ask for éclarcissement; proofs of those discoveries, I have imparted to you. Your doubts are excuseable; but I cannot answer your demands. I could have done it a short time since. I conceive matters more easily than I can describe them: and my mind, more docile than my hand, found evidence where it now finds only uncertainty. Two days since, I was convinced that the earth was round; at present I am persuaded that it is flat. Of those two ideas my mind can form but one that is indubitable; which is, that it cannot be at the same time both round and flat. It is frequently thus that error leads to evidence.

dence. The fun turns rounds the earth, one of thofe men they call philofophers faid to me a few days fince, I believed it, for he convinced me that it was true. Another came and told me the contrary. I fent for the former, and determined to be the judge between them. By what could I learn from thefe difputes, it is poffible that either the one, or the other planet, may make the revolution* : and that the anceftor of one of the difputants was an Alguafil.

You here fee all that I have learned from my acquaintance with this rank of men, whofe fcience at firft aftonifhed me. The particular regard with which they are treated, is one of thofe things that furprife me. Is it not poffible that a people fo enlightened, can hold a fet of men in fuch high efteem, for having no other merit than that of thinking? Certainly they muft look upon reafon as fomething very wonderful. A man has a fingular way of thinking; fpeaks little; laughs never; reafons always; is proud, though poor; unable to purchafe fine clothes, he diftinguifhes himfelf by his rags. That man is a philofopher, and has a right to be infolent.—Another, who is young, would turn philofophy into a court-lady. He dreffes her in gorgeous apparel, and tricks her up with paint and powder: fhe is a laughing coquet, and perfumes announce her approach. They who have been ufed to judge by appearances no longer know her. The philofopher appears to them to be a fool. To fufpect him of thought would be to fuppofe that philofophy was not conftantly one and the fame thing. 'Zais 'had the vapours,' faid Alonzo; 'fhe muft affign 'a pretext for it. Philofophy appeared a plaufible 'one to Zais. She omitted nothing that might make 'her pafs for a philofopher. She foon began to think

* Our author was either ignorant of this matter, or reprefents it badly; for that the earth moves round the fun is as demonftrable to any man of common fenfe, how unlearned foever you may fuppofe him to be, as that either of them move at all.

'herfelf

' herself qualified. Caprice, misanthropy, and pride,
' justified her right to that title. Nothing now was
' wanting, but to find a lover who was as singular as
' herself. She has succeeded.'

Zais and her lover compose an academy. Their
castle is an observatory. Though already far advanced in life, Zais, when in her garden is Flora; in
her balcony she is Urania. Of her lover, aukward as
well as whimsical, she has made a Celadon. What is
there wanting to so ridiculous a scene? Spectators.
Philosophy, Kanhuiscap, is here less the art of think-
king, than a singular way of thinking. All the world
are philosophers. To appear to be so, however, is
not, as you see, a very easy matter.

LETTER XVIII.

*To the same : some customs of the Spaniards with regard
to their women. Amours of their nuns.*

OF all that strikes my wondering sight, Kanhuiscap,
nothing surprises me more, than the behaviour of the
Spaniards towards their wives. The great care they
take to conceal them under an immense heap of clothes,
almost inclines me to think that they are rather ravishers than husbands. By what other motive can they
be influenced, but by a fear least the lawful owners
should reclaim what they have stolen from them? For
what shame can men find in possessing the gifts of love?
These barbarians are ignorant of the pleasures of being seen in the company of those they love: of shewing to the whole universe the delicacy of their choice,
or the value of their conquest : to burn in public those
fires which were kindled in private; and to communicate to a thousand hearts, that homage due to beauty
which one alone can never sufficiently pay. Zilia!
O my dearest Zilia! Ye gods, unjust and cruel! Why
do you yet deprive me of her sight? My looks, united
with

with her's by tendernefs and delight, fhould teach thefe
unfeeling mortals, that there are no ornaments more
precious than the chains of love. I believe, however,
that jealoufy is the motive that induces the Spaniards
fo to conceal their wives ; or rather that it is the perfidy of the women, that forces their hufbands to this
tyranny. The conjugal oath is that which is the moft
readily fworn ; can we then be furprifed that it is fo
little regarded? There are every day to be feen here,
two rich heirs, who unite without affection, live together without love, and feparate without regret.—
Though this ftate may appear to you to be attended
with little anxiety, it is, however, in itfelf unfortunate.   To be loved by a wife is not a happinefs ;
but it is an unhappinefs to be hated by her.

Virginity, which is enjoined by their religion, is
not more fcrupuloufly regarded than conjugal fidelity,
or at moft it is only fo in appearance.   There are
here, as in the city of the Sun, virgins who devote
themfelves to the Deity. They converfe with the
men, however, in a familiar manner. A grate only
feparates them. Now the ufe of this feparation I am
not able to comprehend. For if they have ftrength
enough to preferve their virtue in the midft of the continual intercourfe they have with the men, of what ufe
is the grate : and if love takes poffeffion of their hearts,
what a weak obftacle is fuch an exciting feparation, which gives the eyes leave to act, and the heart
to fpeak ! A fort of Cucipatas are affiduous in their
attendance on thofe virgins, whom they call nuns ;
and under the pretence of infpiring them with a pure
worfhip, they excite and encourage in them, thofe
fentiments of love, to which they become a prey.
Art, which appears to be banifhed from their hearts,
is not, however, from their looks and geftures. A
certain manner which is to be affumed with the veil,
an humble mien, and a ftudied attitude, are fufficient
to employ, during the fourth part of a year, the time,
the pains, and even the vigils of a nun. The eyes

of these religious are also more skilful than those of others.—They are pictures in which we see painted all the sentiments of the heart. Tenderness, innocence, languor, rage, grief, despair, and pleasure, are all there expressed : and if the curtain be dropped over the painting for a moment, it is only to give time to substitute another picture in its place. What difference between the last look of a religious, and that which succeeds it ! All this artifice is, however, nothing more than the work of one man. A Cucipatas has the direction of a mansion filled with nuns ; who are all desirous of pleasing him. They become coquettes ; and their director, how dull soever he may naturally be, is forced to assume an air of coquetry ; gratitude obliges him to it. Sure to please, he contrives fresh means to make himself beloved : he succeeds, and becomes, in a manner, to be adored. You will judge by the following instances. I am informed that one of these virgins has adorned the head of the image of the God of the Spaniards with the hair of a monk. They have also shewn me part of a letter written by a nun to father T ... of which the following is nearly the contents.

' O Jesus ! my father, how unjust you are ! God is
' my witness, that father Ange does not occupy my
' thoughts one moment ; and far from being elevated
' by his sermon, even to an ecstasy (as you reproach
' me) I was during his whole discourse employed with
' thinking of nothing but you. Yes, father, one
' single word from you makes more impression on my
' heart, on that heart which you so little know, than
' all that father Ange could say for whole years to-
' gether ; even though it were in the little parlour of
' our Abbess, and that he thought he was talking
' with her ..... If my eyes seemed to sparkle, it was
' because I was with you when he preached. O that
' you could penetrate to my heart, that you might
' better understand what I write to you. You came
' into the parlour likewise, and never enquired after
' me.

' me. Have you forgot me then? Do you no longer
' remember that ..... You never once regarded me
' yesterday during your whole visit. Will heaven so
' far increase my affliction as to deprive me of the
' consolations I receive from you? For mercy's sake,
' dear father, do not abandon me in that distress you
' have now plunged me into. I deserve your pity: and
' if you have not compassion on me, you will soon
' hear no more of the unfortunate Theresa. You will
' receive from the keeper of our turning-box an al-
' mond cake of my making. I have inclosed, in this
' letter, a billet that sister A ...... wrot. to father
' don X ...... I found means to intercept it; and I
' think it will afford you some entertainment. Oh!
' that ..... The bell rings. Adieu.' After t. is,
Kanhuiscap, you cannot refrain from allowing that
the Spaniards are as ridiculous in their armours, as
they are remorseless in their cruelties. It is only
in the house of Alonzo, I believe, that justice and
reason prevail. I am not able to determine, however,
what I should think of the behaviour of Zulmira: it
is too tender to be the effect of art alone, and too
studied to proceed from the heart.

LETTER XIX.

*To the same: reflections of Aza on the futility of meta-
physical knowledge.*

TO think is a profession: to know oneself is an ac-
complishment. It is not given to every man, Kanhuiscap, to read his own heart. There is a certain rank of philosophers here, who alone have that
right, or rather that of confounding this knowledge.
Far from endeavouring to correct the passions, their
only concern is to know from whence they proceed:
and this science, which ought to make the bad man
blush, serves only to make them see that they have one

qualification

qualification the more; which is, the unfruitful talent
of knowing their own imperfections. The meta-
physicians, for that is the name of these philosophers,
distinguish in man three principles; the foul, the mind,
and the heart; and all their science only tends to
know from which of these such or such an action
proceeds. This discovery once made, their arro-
gance becomes inconceivable. Virtue is not, so to
speak, any longer made for them; they think it
sufficient to know what it is that produces it; and frequently resemble those who are disgusted with a liquor
that is excellent in itself, when they know that it
comes from a country that is but little esteemed.

From the same cause it is, that the metaphysician,
intoxicated with a science that he thinks wonderful,
omits no opportunity of displaying his knowledge. If
he writes to his mistress, his letter is nothing more
than a precise analysis of the minutest faculties of his
foul. His mistress thinks herself obliged to reply in
the fame style; and they confounded each other with
chimerical distinctions and expressions, which custom
has authorised, though it has not rendered intelligible.
Your own reflections on the manners of the Spaniards,
will easily lead you to those which I have here made.
Would that my heart were free, my generous friend!
I could then paint with more force these thoughts,
which have here no other order than that which my
present agitation will allow.—The time approaches
when my miseries will have an end. Zilia will at
length appear to my impatient sight. The thought
of that pleasure disorders my reason. I fly to meet
her. I behold her participate of my anxieties and
my pleasures: the tender tears flow from our eyes.
Again united after our misfortunes.....How is my
foul afflicted, Kanhuifcap! in what a horrid state will
she find me! the wretched slave of a barbarian, whose
fetters perhaps she bears, at the court of a haughty
conqueror. Can she remember her lover? Can she
think that he still lives? She is in bondage: can she
imagine

imagine that obstacles sufficiently strong, have been able ..... Kanhuiscap, what ought I to expect? What lot is reserved for me? When I was worthy of her, cruel gods! you snatched her from my arms. Shall I only find her again to be a fresh witness of my ignominy? And thou, barbarous element, which art to restore me the object of my love, canst thou restore me to my glory?

LETTER XX.

To the same : the despair of Aza, who imagines ZILIA *to have been swallowed up by the sea.*

WHAT cruel power has snatched me from the darkness of the grave? What ungracious pity has made me again behold the detested light? Kanhuiscap, my misfortunes increase with my days, and my strength augments with the excess of my misery ..... Zilia is no more! ..... O horrid despair! O cruel remembrance! Zilia is no more! and I still breath! and these hands, which grief should bind, can still form those knots which misery attends, which tears bedew, and which are conveyed to thee by despair. In vain has the sun performed a third part of his course, since you pierced my heart with that most fatal stroke. In vain has despondency, a total dejection, possessed my soul even to this day. My grief, ineffectually restrained, has become only the more violent. I have lost my Zilia. An immense space of time seemed to separate us ; and at this moment I lose her for ever. The dreadful stroke that snatched her from me ; the perfidious element that surrounds her, present themselves to my distracted sight. I see my Zilia borne on the hideous waves ..... the sun retires with horror behind the thickest clouds ; the sea opens to hide its crime from that god : but it cannot conceal her from me. Through the waters I behold the body of Zilia :

Q 3

her

her eyes . . . . . her bolom . . . . . a livid palenets . . . . .
O my friend . . . . . inexorable death . . . . . death that
flies from me . . . . . Ye gods, more cruel in your indulgence than in your punifhments! Why do ye ftill
fulfer me to live? Will you never unite thofe whom
you cannot feporate? In vain, Kanhuifcap, do I call
on death : he flies from me : the barbarian is deaf to
my voice, and keeps his darts for thofe that would
avoid them. Zilia, my beloved Zilia, hear my cries;
behold my flowing tears ; thou haft none; I only live
to fhed them : O that I could drown myfelf in the
torrent that flows from my eyes . . . . . why can I not?
. . . . Ah! you have none; foul of my foul! You . . . .
my hands will no longer lend me their aid I
fink under my affliction . . . . horrid defpair . . . . tears
. . . . love . . . . a ftrange coldnefs . . . . Zilia . . . . Kanhuifcap . . . . Zilia! . . . .

LETTER XXI.

To the fame: AZA *recovers from a dangerous illnefs
by the cares of* ALONZO *and* ZULMIRA.

WHAT will be your aftonifhment, Kanhuifcap,
when thefe knots which my hands are fcarce able to
form, fhall tell you that I ftill live. My grief, my
defpair, the time that has pafled fince you have heard
from me, all muft have convinced you that I no longer
exifted. Difmifs thofe anxieties which are due to
friendfhip, efteem, and misfortune ; and let not my
weaknefs make you deplore my prefent exiftence : the
the lofs of Zilia ought to have finifhed my being.
The gods, who fhou'd have pardoned me the crime of
feeking my death, have taken from me the power of
committing it. Subdued by grief, fcarcely did I perceive the approach of death, who came at laft to put
a period to my miferies. A dangerous difeafe laid
hold of me, and would have led me to the tomb, if
the

the unfortunate interpofitions of Alonzo had not pro-
tracted my duration. I breathe: but it is only to
be a prey to the molt cruel anxieties. In that herrid
ftate I now am; all things diiguft me. The friendihip
of Alonzo, the grief of Zulmira, their attention, their
tears, all afflict me. Alone in the midft of mankind,
I only difcern thofe that furround me, to fly from
them. May a friend lefs unfortunate, Kanhuifcap,
be the recompenſe of thy virtue! I am too diſtracted
a lover to be a rational friend: for how can I tafte
the fweets of friendihip, when I am oppreſſed by love
with the molt cruel torments?

LETTER XXII.

To the fame: Alonzo and Zulmira endeavour to
diſſipate the grief of Aza.

Friendship, at length, has reſtored me to thee,
Kanhuiſcap; to myſelf. Too much corcerned at my
afflictions, Alonzo would diſſipate, or at leaſt ſhare them
with me. With this defign he carried me to a coun-
try-feat he has a few miles from Madrid. There I
found the fatisfaction of meeting with nothing that did
not anfwer to the dejection of my mind. A wood, in
the neighbourhood of Alonzo's villa, has been a long
time the fecret depofitory of my woes. There I faw
no objects but what were proper to nourifh my defpondency. Frightful rocks: enormous mountains,
defpoiled of their verdure; thick ſtreams flow facing
over their muddy beds; dark pines, whofe mournful
branches feem to touch the clouds; fcorched grafs,
and withered flowers; adders and croaking ravens;
were the only witneffes of my tears. Alonzo foon
took me, regardlefs of my entreaties, from thefe
gloomy fcenes. It was then that I found how much
misfortunes are alleviated by participation; and
how much I owed to the tender cares of Zulmira and
Alonzo.

Alonzo. Where shall I find colours strong enough,
Kanhuiscap, to paint the grief that my unhappiness
occasioned them? Zulmira, the tender Zulmira, graced
them with her tears ; her affliction was but little less
than my own. Pale and dejected, whenever her eyes
met mine, they flowed with grief; while Alonzo tenderly deplored my unhappy fate.

LETTER XXIII. •

To the same : Zulmira *is in love with* Aza ; *the
incidents that attend it.*

Zulmira, whose cares all centred in the unhappiness of Aza ; Zulmira, who participated my griefs,
and trembled for my life ; is now herself on the brink
of the grave : every moment augments her dangers,
and threatens her dissolution. Yielding at last to the
tender intreaties of her father, who lay groaning at .
her feet, without hopes of affording her any relief;
and perhaps still more influenced by the emotions of
her heart, Zulmira spoke. It is I, it is Aza, whom
misfortune will never forsake ; it is that wretch, whose
distracted heart knows nothing but despair ; and the
mass of whose blood is changed by love into a baneful
poison, who is the cause of this misfortune. It is I
that have taken Zulmira from her father, from my
friend. She loves me ; she dies. Alonzo follows her.
Zilia is no more ! ' I have felt for thy griefs; come and
' partake of mine' (said the distracted father to me.)
' Come and give me back my life, and my child.
' Wretched man, whose miseries I lament at the very
' moment I entreat you to alleviate my own. Be sen-
' sible to friendship; for it is yet in your power.
' The most amiable of all virtues cannot injure your
' love. Come follow me!' At these words, which were
accompanied by deep-fetched sighs, he led me to the
apartment of his daughter. With horror and dejection,

jection, I tremblingly entered. The paleness of death
was fpread over her countenance: but her darkened
eyes were re-animated at the fight of me: my prefence feemed to give new life to the unfortunate
Zulmira.

'I die,' fhe faid to me with faltering accents: 'I
'never fhall fee you more: that is all my grief. At
'leaft, Aza, while I yet live fuffer me to fay I
'love you. I can .... Yes, remember that Zul-
'mira carries with her to the grave that love which
'fhe could not conceal: that which her looks, her
'actions have fo often declared; and which your in-
'difference has at laft ..... but I cannot reproach
'you: your fenfibility would have proved your in-
'conftancy. Devoted to another, death alone can
'feparate you: it never can diveft me of the love I
'bear you. I prefer it to the cure of a mifery that
'I cherifh: Of a mifery .... Aza ....' She ftretch-
ed her hand towards me: her fpirits left her; fhe fell;
her eyes clofed: but while I reproached myfelf with
her death, and added my anxieties to thofe of her de-
fpairing father; the cares of others had brought her
back to life. Her eyes opened again, and though ftill
darkened with defpondency, fhe fixed them on me, and
expreffed the moft tender love. 'Aza! Aza!' fhe
faid again, 'do not hate me.' I fell at her feet,
overcome by her diftrefs. A fudden joy fhone in her
countenance: but unable to bear the various emotions
her mind fuftained, fhe again fainted under them.
They forced me away, to fave her from a repetition
of fuch dangerous agitations. What can you think,
Kanhuifcap, of thefe new misfortunes to which I am
a prey: of that mifery which I caufe to thofe to whom
I owe the greateft obligations? This new grief is come
to add itfelf to thofe which attend me in the gloomy
defert, where love, defpair, and death were my conftant companions.

LETTER

LETTER XXIV.

To the same: ZULMIRA *is reſtored her to health.*

MY friend, the lot of Alonzo is changed. The grief by which he was oppreſſed has given place to joy. Zulmira, ready to deſcend to the grave, is re-ſtored to life. It is no longer that Zulmira whom languor had reduced to the brink of diſſolution: her eyes, reanimated, now diſplay that beauty and thoſe graces, with which her youth is adorned. Though I admire her reviving charms, can you believe it? far from talking to me of her love, ſhe ſeems, on the con-trary, to be confounded by the confeſſion that has eſcaped her. Her looks are caſt down whenever her eyes meet mine. My pains were ſuſpended; but alas! how ſhort the ſuſpenſe. Zilia, my deareſt Zilia, can I be diverted from my grief? Forgive thoſe moments that I have ſtolen from thee: all that yet remain ſhall be conſecrated to my misfortunes. Do not imagine, Kanhuiſcap, that the fear which Alonzo has ſhewn me for Zulmira, can ſhake my conſtancy. In vain does he repreſent to me the empire of Aza over the heart of his daughter: the joy that our union would give him; and the death that muſt follow our ſeparation. I remain ſilent before that unhappy father. My heart, faithful to my paſſion, is firm, determined for Zilia. No; in vain does Alonzo, ready to depart for that unfortunate country, which ſhall never more behold my Zilia, offer me that power which his unjuſt king has given him over my people. It would be to ac-knowledge a tyrant, to avail myſelf of his power. My hands may be loaded with irons, but they ſhall never enchain my heart. For ever will I entertain for the barbarous chief of the Spaniards, that hatred which I owe to the firſt among a people who have been the cauſe of all my miſeries, and thoſe of my unhappy country.

LETTER

LETTER XXV.

To the same : AZA *contrives the design of espousing* ZUL- MIRA. *He gives the reasons that induces him to it.*

MY eyes are opened, Kanhuifcap: the flames of love yield, without being extinguished, to the torch of reafon. O immortal flames that devour my bofom! Zilia! thou of whofe image nothing can deprive me : thou whom a fatal deftiny has fnatched from me for ever; be not offended, if the defire of feeking vengeance for you, excites me to betray you. No longer tell me, Kanhuifcap, of what I owe to my people and my father. I no longer talk of the tyranny of the Spaniards. Can I forget my misfortunes and their crimes? They have coft me too dear. That cruel remembrance roufes my fury. It is done : I confent! I go to unite myfelf with Zulmira. Alonzo, I have given thee that promife. Can it be a crime to leave Zulmira in poffeffion of an error that is pleafing to her ? She thinks that fhe triumphs over my heart. Ah! far from undeceiving her, let her enjoy her imaginary happinefs : let her . . . . . It is by this means only that I can avenge my oppreffed people and myfelf. No fooner fhall our union be accomplifhed, than I fhall depart for the land of the Sun; that defolated country, whofe miferies you defcribe to me. It is there that I fhall purfue that vengeance whofe violent tranfports I now fupprefs. It is on a perfidious people that I will hurl my fury. Reduced to the bafe condition of a wretched flave; and for the firft time forced to diffemble, I go to punifh the Spaniards for for my deception, and for their offences : while the family of Alonzo fhall enjoy all that the grateful heart can beftow, and all thofe homages which are due to virtue.

LETTER

LETTER XXVI.

To the same : on sincerity in religion.

IF you were one of thofe men who are conducted by
prejudice, I fhould imagine what would be your furprife, when you was told by an Inca, that he no longer
adored the Sun.   I fhould hear you complain to
that ftar of the light which he ftill afforded me ; and
to thyfelf for the trouble you took in communicating
your fentiments.   You would be aftonifhed, that,
perjured to my God, friendfhip, that virtue of which˙
the vicious have no conception, could ftill dwell in my
breaft.   But, fortified againft thofe prejudices which
were taught you as virtues, you require of a Peruvian
nothing but the love of his country, of virtue, and of
freedom.   I expect from you more juft reproaches.
You will, perhaps, be furprifed, and with reafon, to
fee me abandon a worfhip that appeared to me irra-
tional, and at the fame time appear zealous for a religion of which I have pointed out to you the contradictions.   I have already made that objection to myfelf : but it prefently vanifhed, when I was informed
that the law which I have had the audacity to cenfure, was dictated by that God who was the author
of our being ! In fact, of what confequence is the particular form of any worfhip, provided it be enjoined
by him to whom it is rendered ?   On this principle it
is, that I do not blufh to conform to thofe ceremonies
which I have formerly condemned.   How great, how
awful are the works of the Supreme Being! Could
you read, Kanhuifcap, thofe divine books that have
been communicated to me, what wifdom, what power,
what immenfity, would you there difcover !   You
would there readily difcern the hand of the Divinity.
Thofe unfurmountable contradictions which I at firft
found in the difpenfations of that power, are here evidently

dently juftified. It is not the fame, however, with regard to the conduct of thefe men toward their God.

Do not imagine, credulous as we commonly are, I wrote you this upon the report of a prieft only. I have too much experienced the fallehood of our Cucipatas, to credit the fables of thofe who refemble them. The high rank which they hold among all nations, induces them to practife deceit: for their grandeur is frequently founded on nothing but the errors of ambitious people: it would be too dear a purchafe for them, if the empire of the world was to be obtained by virtue only: they are much better pleafed to obtain it by impofture.

LETTER XXVII.

To the fame: the diftraction of Aza, *who is on the point of marrying* Zulmira.

IT is done, Kanhuifcap: Zulmira now attends me. I go to the altar. You fee me already there: but do you fee the remorfe that attends me! Do you behold the altars tremble at the fight of a perjurer? The fhade of Zilia, bloody and indignant, enlightens thefe nuptials with a mournful torch; and with a reproaching tone fhe fays, 'Is this the faith that you have ' fworn to me? Perfidious! Is this the love that ' fhould reanimate my afhes? You love me, you fay, ' and yet you give your hand to Zulmira. You love ' me, traitor, and yet you give to another that blefs- ' ing which I could never enjoy! Did I yet live....' What tortures, Kanhuifcap, rend my breaft? I hear the injured Zulmira demand a heart to which fhe has a lawful right. I behold my father and my people bending under a cruel yoke, and calling on me to be their deliverer. I then remember my promife...... I go to fulfil it.

R.   LETTER

LETTER XXVIII.

To the same : AZA, *informed of the arrival of* ZILIA *in France, leaves* ALONZO *and* ZULMIRA *to go to her.*

ZILIA ſtill lives! Where can I find a meſſenger ſwift enough to communicate to you the exceſs of my joy ? Kanhuiſcap, you who have felt my griefs, participate of the tranſports of my ſoul. O that the flames which now grow in my breaſt, could fly and impart to thine the overflowings of my felicity. The ſea ; our enemies ; death ; no, nothing has taken from me the object of my love. She lives! ſhe loves me! think then what are my tranſports! Brought into a neighbouring ſtate, into France, Zilia has experienced no misfortune but that of our ſeparation, and of the uncertainty of my ſtate. How do the gods protect the virtuous! A generous Frenchman has delivered her from the barbarity of the Spaniards. All things were ready to unite me with Zulmira; I was going, O ye gods! . . . . . when I heard that Zilia ſtill lived, and that ſhe would ſhortly be with me. No obſtacle can keep her from me. I ſhall again behold her. From her lips ſhall I hear thoſe tender ſentiments, which her hands have traced ; and at her feet I ſhall . . . . O Heavens, I tremble at the thought of that which is the cauſe of all my joy. My happineſs confounds me. Zilia is coming into the midſt of her enemies! New dangers! . . . . . She ſhall not come. I will fly to prevent her. What can hinder me ? The gods have diſengaged me from Alonzo and Zulmira. —Zilia ſtill lives. I receive her from the hands of virtue. In vain did gratitude, eſteem, and friendſhip, eſpouſe the cauſe of Deterville her deliverer ; ſhe oppoſed to them our love, and obliged them to yield to our flames. Glorious combat! How do I admire that effort! Deterville ſtifles his love : he for-

g ts

gets the rights which he had over her: and behold his generofity; he unites us for ever. Zilia! Zilia! I go to drink deep of felicity. I fly to meet her, to behold her, and to die with pleafure at her feet.

LETTER XXIX.

To the fame: AZA *is jealous of* DETERVILLE, *and from what motive.*

YOU muft accufe Zilia only, dear friend, for my filence. I have feen her; and I have feen nothing but her. Do not expect that I fhould exprefs to you thofe tranfports, thofe ravifhing delights in which I was abforbed the firft moment fhe appeared to my fight. To conceive them it were neceffary to love Zilia as I love her. Muft torments yet unknown invade a felicity fo pure? Between the bofom of pleafure and the den of grief is there then no interval? After fuch voluptuous delights, a thoufand tortures tear my heart. My tendernefs is odious to me; and at the moment that I would not love, I am poffeffed with all its fury. I have borne the grief that the lofs of Zilia occafioned; I cannot bear that which I now feel. She loves me no more . . . . . O diftracting thought! When I behold her, love pours into my foul, with one hand pleafure, and with the other torture. In the firft tranfports of a happinefs fo pure, that I cannot exprefs to you the fweetnefs that attended it, Zilia ftole from my arms to read a letter, which was given her by the young perfon who had conducted me hither. Difordered, afflicted, melted, thofe tears which fhe had juft given to joy, no longer flowed but for grief. She bathed that letter with her tears. Her grief made me anxious for her welfare. The ingrate tafted pleafures. The grief of which I had partaken was the triumph of my rival. Deterville, that deliverer, whofe praife the letters of Zilia

had

had fo frequently repeated, had written that. It was
dictated by the moft lively paffion. By retiring from
Zilia, after having given her up to his rival, he had
completed his own generofity and her affliction. She
explained to me, with vivacity, expreffions that were
more than acknowledgments. She forced me to admire thofe virtues, which at that cruel moment gave
me mortal wounds. My grief then fought aid from
a determined indifference. I foon abfented myfelf
from Zilia. Filled with defpair, from which nothing
can deliver me, every reflection that I make is a new
mifery. It takes from me my hope, my comfort. I
have loft the heart of Zilia. That heart . . . . . I cannot bear the thought. My rival will be happy!
Ah! It is too much to think that he deferves that
happinefs.

Frightful jealoufy? Thy cruel ferpents have ftolen
upon my heart. A thoufand fears: Black fufpicions
. . . . . Zilia, her virtues, her tendernefs, her beauty:
my injuftice perhaps; all agitate, all torment me. I
am loft. It is vain that my grief conceals itfelf under an apparent tranquillity. Fain would I fpeak,
complain, accufe, and yet I am filent. What can I
fay to Zilia? Can I reproach her with having infpired
Deterville with a love that proceeds from virtue? She
does not enjoy his tendernefs. But why heap on him
thofe praifes? Why inceffantly repeating his eulogy?
. . . . . Love, thou fource of my pleafures, oughteft
thou to be that of my miferies?

LETTER XXX.

To the same : AZA's *jealousy increases: he believes* ZILIA *to be unfaithful.*

WHERE am I, Kanhuiscap? By what torments am I followed? My brain burns with the most cruel fury. Zilia, perfidous Zilia, pale and dejected, laments the absence of my rival. Deterville, by flying, has gained the victory. Heavens! on whom shall my rage fall! He is beloved, Kanhuiicap; all things tell it me. The inhuman does not attempt to conceal her infidelity. Precious remains of innocence ; though she knows her crime, she detests hypocrisy. I read her perjury in her eyes. Her lips even dare to avow it, by repeating incessantly the name that I abhor. Whither shall I fly? When present with Zilia I suffer frightful torments, and absent from her I die.

When, seduced by the sweetness of her looks, she spreads for an instant tranquillity over my mind, I think she loves me. That thought throws me into a rapture that deprives me of reason. I recover myself, and would speak. I begin ; break off; am silent. The sentiments that by turns possess my heart, trouble and confound me. I am unable to exprefs myself. A fatal remembrance ; Deterville ; a sigh from Zilia, re-animates those transports which in vain I would calm. Even the shades of night cannot screen me from their violence. If for a moment I give myself up to sleep, the unfaithful Zilia snatches me from it. I see Deterville at her feet ; she hears him with plea-sure. Frighted sleep flies far from me. The day offers me fresh griefs. For ever devoted to the fury of jealousy, his fires have even dried up my tears. Zilia ! Zilia ! How great the evils that spring from so much love ! I adore thee ; I offend thee : O Heavens ! I lose thee !

LETTER

LETTER XXXI.

To the same : Aza reproaches himself with the effects of his jealousy.

ZILIA, love, Deterville, fatal jealousy! What di-
straction! A cloud hides from me the names I trace.
Kanhuiscap, I no longer know myself: In the fury of
the blackest jealousy, I have armed myself with darts,
with which I have pierced the heart of Zilia.   She had
written to Deterville; the letter was still in her hand.
A fatal moment disordered my reason.   I formed the
most rash project . . . . . . My promise, the religion I
have embraced, all things prompted me.   The most
trifling pretences appeared to me to be as laws of
equity for deserting her. I have pronounced the inhuman sentence. Cruel adieus . . . What a moment . . . .
Could I do it? Yes, Kanhuiscap, I fled from Zilia.
Zilia at my feet, with groans, to which mine were just
ready to reply . . . . . . Deterville! What a remembrance! Possessed with fury, I flew from her arms.
But soon, vainly persisting, I would return to them :
all things oppose : I dare not resist.   Gods! what
have I done? How shameful is the distress! How
horrible the repentance!

LETTER XXXII.

*To the same : Aza falls again into suspicions of Zilia.
Zulmira meditates a signal vengeance.*

CEASE to wonder at my long silence : Could the
cruel state of my heart permit me to inform you sooner
of my fate? Do not think, that distracted by remorse, I still reproach myself with unjust suspicions.
It is Zilia, it is her cruel heart, and not mine, that
they

they ought to devour. Yes, Kanhuilcap, her fighs, her tears, and groans, were nothing but effects of fhame ; traces that virtue, when flying from us, ftill leaves in our hearts. It is to efface them that fhe cruelly refufes to fee me again. Her obftinacy has forced me to a diftance from her. Retired to the extremity of the fame city, unknown to any one, totally devoted to grief and misfortunes, I labour to forget the ingrate I adore. Ufelefs cares! Love, in our defpite, fteals into our hearts, and in our defpite there he cruelly dwells. In vain would I drive him thence. Jealoufy there fupports him: and when I would banifh jealoufy, love keeps him there. The wretched fport of thefe paffions, my foul is divided between tendernefs and rage. Sometimes I reproach my fufpicions, and fometimes my love. Can I be charmed with an ungrateful woman? Can I forget her whom I adore? But whatever may be my love for her, nothing can excufe her. Would fhe had hated me! We can pardon hatred, but never perfidy.

The folicitude and friendfhip of Alonzo have difcovered that retreat, where grief, and all the deftructive evils to which human nature is fubject, has driven me. Zulmira loads me with reproaches. I have juft received her letter. In her eyes I appear as an ungrateful wretch, whom neither promifes nor tears can recal. I have only freed her from the arms of death to deliver her to more cruel torments. She will come, fhe fays, and fignalize in France her fury and my perfidy: avenge her father and her love. Every word of her letter is a dart that pierces my bofom. I know too well the powers of defpair not to fear the effects. Zilia is the unfortunate object of her rage. Bathed in her blood, it is that Zulmira will appear before me. Avenging gods! is it thus that you leave to crimes the care of their punifhments? Hold, Zulmira, on me pour all your fury. Let the apoftate enjoy a life of which remorfe will be the chaftifement. Thus will you indeed fignalize your
vengeance.

vengance?. But O heavens! Zilia in the arms of a
rival. I groan, wretch that I am, and tremble for
her, while the ingrate is betraying me. Oppressed by
the weight of evils, my body sinks under its weakne-
ness; while the perfidious, in triumphing even over
her remorse, recals my rival. Wretch that I am! I
breathe..... I still exist! But what misery to exist
when we only live to suffer.

LETTER XXXIII.

To the same: innocence of ZILIA. *Generosity of* ZUL-
MIRA. *Despair of* AZA.

WHAT have I said? What horror surrounds me?
Learn my shame, Kanhuiscap, and, if it can be, my
remorse, before you know my crime. Odious to myself, I will now expose it to your sight. Cease to lament my misfortunes; and make them complete by
your hatred. Zilia is void of all guilt. To reflect
on it is even an injury to her. You know my suspicions; their injustice will tell you my misery, which
can never have an end: something unlooked for will
for ever arise. After the penity of Zilia, could you
have thought that heaven would have given me over
to new torments? Could you have thought that her
innocence, which ought to make me happy, would
have been to me the source of the most bitter torments? To what errors have I been a prey? What
clouds have obscured my reason? Zilia could deceive
me! I could think it! She will see me no more. My
remembrance is odious to her. She loved me too
much, not to hate me. Abandoned to my horrid
misery, friendship, confidence, nothing can alleviate
my miseries. They will poison thy heart with their
venom, and mine will yet find no relief. In vain
does Zulmira, divested of her fury, tell me that she
has offered it as a sacrifice to my repose and felicity.

Retired

Retired to a houſe of virgins, ſhe has conſecrated to
her God, and to my happineſs, her life, and the
flower of her days. Zulmira, generous Zulmira,
canſt thou renounce thy vengeance? Ah! if thy heart
were cruel, what pleaſure would it find in my horrid
miſeries! It is then only to myſelf, to the baſereſs of
my ſentiments, that I owe the misfortunes which I
endure. Nothing was wanting to make me com-
pletely miſerable, but to be myſelf the cauſe of it:
and behold I am. Zilia loved me; I ſaw it; my
happineſs was ſure. Her tenderneſs! her ſentiments!
my felicity! ought they to have been ſacrificed to a
baſe ſuſpicion? O frightful deſpair! I fled from Zilia.
It was I ..... Generous friend, can you conceive the
ſtate in which I now am? Can I conceive it myſelf?
Remorſe, love, deſpair, contend for my heart, that
they may devour it.

LETTER XXXIV.

To ZILIA: AZA *forces himſelf to a ſubmiſſion, and
acknowledges his injuſtice to* ZILIA.

THE dread of diſpleaſing you ſtill keeps in my trembling hands the knots which I form. Theſe knots
which were once conſolation and joy to you, Zilia,
are now twined by grief and deſpair. Do not imagine that I would conceal my crime from your eyes.
Diſtracted with anxiety for having believed you unfaithful, how ſhould I preſume to juſtify it? But am
I not ſufficiently puniſhed? What remorſe! ......
The remorſe of a lover who adores you. Ah! you
would hate me! Have I not rather merited your contempt than your hatred? Reflect for a moment on all
my misfortunes. Barbarians ſnatched thee from my
love, at the moment it ſhould have been crowned with
ſucceſs. Armed for thy defence, I fell, and was
loaded with their baſe fetters. Carried to their country,

try, the waves on which we floated, supported for a time, it is true, all my hopes. I lived only by them. My heart went with you. Thy ravishers being swallowed up by the sea, plunged me into the most cruel error. That which I thought had destroyed thee, could not destroy my love. Grief augmented my passion. I would have died to follow thee. I only lived to avenge thee. All things I essayed. Even my very oaths I would have sacrificed, and have united myself, in defiance of a thousand remorses, with a Spanish woman, and have purchased at that price, my liberty and my vengeance. When on a sudden, O unhoped for felicity! I learned that you lived, and that you still loved me. O too pleasing remembrance! I flew to thee; to happiness the most pure, the most ecstatic . . . . . Ah! vain hope : cruel reverse! Scarcely had I enjoyed the first transports with which thy sight inspired me, than a fatal poison, of which thy heart is too pure to know the pangs; jealousy seized my soul : his most rancorous serpents have devoured my heart; that heart which was only formed for the love of thee. The most amiable of virtues, gratitude, was the object of my suspicions. That which you owed to Deterville, I thought he had obtained : that your virtue had been confounded with your duty. I thought . . . . . It was these fatal ideas that troubled our first transports. You was unable, even in the bosom of love, to forget friendship. I forgot virtue. The eulogies of Deterville; his letter; the sentiments it expressed : the concern it gave you : the grief you shewed for the loss of your deliverer; all these I attributed to the sentiments that I felt, and that I still feel, to love.

I concealed in my bosom the fires that consumed it. What was the consequence? From suspicion I soon passed to a certainty of your perfidy. I meditated even a punishment for it. I would not employ reproaches : I did not think you worthy of them. I
will

wil. · · endeavour to conceal my crimes from you : truth. · · n as dear to me as my love.

I v c · · turn to Spain to perform a promife to which i. · om.er oath had engaged me. Repentance foon fello. ed that rage which had declared to you my crime. I vainly endeavoured to deceive you, with re_.d to a refolution that love had deftroyed almoft as foon as it was formed. Thy determination not to fee me re丶urn'd my fury. Again given up to jealoufy ; I fled from you ; but far from going to Madrid to confummate a crime that my foul detefted ; though you was induced to believe it : finking under the weight of my misfortunes, I fought in folitude, in an eftrangement from mankind, that peace which tranquillity of mind alone can afford. Overcome by my diftrefs, the powers of life forfook me. A long time abfent from thee, fhall I, in fpite of myfelf, avow it to thee, Zilia? All my faculties were exerted in reviling thee. I thought I faw you, pleafed with my flight, recal my rival. I thought I faw . . . . . Alas ! you know my offence ; but you do not know my punifhment : it even furpaffes my crime. Ah Zilia, if the excefs of love could effect it : no, I can no more be guilty. Do not imagine that I intend to move thy pity ; that were too little for my tendernefs. Zilia, give me back your love, or give me nothing. Liften to the love that ought ftill to fpeak in thy heart : fuffer me in thy prefence again to relumine that fire which thy juft refentment has extinguifhed. Some fpark may yet be found in the afhes of that love which you once nourifhed for Aza. Zilia, Zilia, thou director of my fate ; I have confefled to thee my crime. If thy pardon doth not efface it, it muft ftill be punifhed. My death fhall be the chaftifement. Too happy, inexorable ! if at leaft I can expire at thy feet !

LETTER XXXV.

To K ANHUISCAP: ZILIA *gives up her heart to* ALA. *Their approaching return to their native country.*

WOULD that by ftriking thy mind with furprife, I could communicate to thy heart that joy with which mine now pants. O happinefs! O tranfport! Kanhuifcap, Zilia has given me up her heart. She loves me. Roving in the ravifhments of my love, I fhed at her feet the moft tender tears. Her looks, her fighs, her tranfports, are the only interpreters of our love and our felicity. Imagine, if you can, our joys: that moment conftantly prefents to my fight; that moment . . . . No, fuch love, angnifh, and delight, are not to be expreffed by words. Her eyes, her animated countenance, told me her love, her anger, my fhame . . . She turned pale. Faint, and fpeechlefs, fhe funk into my arms. But as the flames excited by the winds, fo my heart, agitated by fear, burnt with greater violence. My head reclining on her bofom, I breathed that fire of love which animated her life, and united it with mine. She died and inftantly revived . . . . Zilia, my beloved Zilia! Into what intoxicating pleafures haft thou plunged the happy Aza! No, Kanhuifcap, you can never conceive our happinefs: come and bear witnefs to it. Nothing fhould be wanting to my felicity. The Frenchman who delivers you this letter will bring you hither. You will then behold my Zilia. My felicity will every moment increafe. The ftory of our prefent happinefs, as well as that of our paft misfortunes (far be they removed from us!) has reached even to the throne. The generous monarch of the French nation, has ordered certain fhips that are going to encounter with the Spaniards in our feas, to carry us to Guitto. We foon again fhall fee our native land; that mournful country, fo dear to our

desires :

defires : thofe abodes, O Zilia ! where fprang our firft delights, thy fighs and mine. May they be witneffes ! may they celebrate ! may they augment ! if it be poffible, our prefent felicity ...But I go to Zilia. My dear friend, love cannot make me forget friendfhip, but friendfhip keeps me too long from love. Thofe delightful tranfports that ravifh my foul, it is in thy enjoyments that I have again found life .... I am loft in the excefs of happinefs; in ecftatic blifs ! Zilia is again my own ; fhe waits my coming ; I fly to her arms !

S

THE END.

ASPIN, Printer,
Lombard-Street, Fleet-Street.

www.ingramcontent.com/pod-product-compliance
Lightning Source LLC
Chambersburg PA
CBHW020615030726
47497CB00007B/2248